★

If I remained perfectly still, no one could be sure I was there.

The dark presence crept slowly along the cliff, staying behind the low bank of shrubs, never shifting its gaze from my house. A prickle of fear touched the back of my neck. This didn't appear to be someone from Millicent's party—a guest strolling the grounds or admiring the view of the lake. This was a malevolent presence, a stalker in the shadows, a frightening apparition, perhaps connected somehow to the skeleton in the cistern, someone who had killed once and might easily kill again.

And that presence was staring straight down at my window.

★

SECRETS
DARK AND DEEP

ANNE WHITE

W⊕RLDWIDE®

TORONTO • NEW YORK • LONDON
AMSTERDAM • PARIS • SYDNEY • HAMBURG
STOCKHOLM • ATHENS • TOKYO • MILAN
MADRID • WARSAW • BUDAPEST • AUCKLAND

To the Tuesday and Thursday Water Aerobics Class at the Glens Falls YMCA, the most loyal and supportive group of readers any writer could hope to find, and to our unbelievably patient teacher Phyllis Hudson and her talented daughter, Alexis, who pull out all the stops to turn book signings into very special events.

Recycling programs
for this product may
not exist in your area.

SECRETS DARK AND DEEP

A Worldwide Mystery/April 2009

First published by Hilliard & Harris.

ISBN-13: 978-0-373-26669-2
ISBN-10:   0-373-26669-3

Printed in U.S.A.

My sincere thanks to:

Stephanie and Shawn Reilly of Hilliard and Harris for accepting and publishing my Lake George Mystery Series; Matt Witten, Supervising Producer for the CW Show Supernatural, for being an extraordinary teacher and adviser; Suzanne Merrill for offering her friendship and moral support, for answering a hundred and one questions about present-day books and authors and for patiently unraveling the mysteries of grammar and punctuation for me; Doris Quick for her help in finding an appropriate title and for sharing a wealth of ideas and information on writing; The Malice Domestic organization for awarding me an Unpublished Writers' Grant in 1999 and a Malice Domestic Best First Mystery Nomination in 2002; John Strong, Executive Director; Laura Von Rosk, Gallery Director; and members of the Lake George Arts Project for outstanding writing workshops; Nathalie Costa and the dedicated people at the Adirondack Center for Writing for their assistance and encouragement to area authors; LARAC, The Lower Adirondack Regional Arts Council; Patricia Joyce, longtime Executive Director (now retired); Ellen C. Butz, current Executive Director; Anne Smoczynski, Grants and Membership Director; Patrice Jarvis-Weber, Administrative Assistant; and Diane Swanson, Gallery Director, for their ongoing support of writers; The Unusual Suspects Mystery Writers, my Saratoga Springs writers' group, always ready with helpful critiques and suggestions; Kim and Mike Smith at Dog Ate My Homework and Susan Fox and Naftali Rottenstreich at Red Fox Books for bringing two bookstores to downtown Glens Falls, something which for many years had been beyond our wildest hopes; And last, but by no means least, my husband Charles, and my children Kate, Michael, James, Richard, Charles H. and Steven and their families for their continuing love and encouragement.

ONE

I SHOULD HAVE KNOWN BETTER.

Actually, I did know better. That's what made it so hard to understand how one simple blunder could snowball into the kind of problem I'd been determined to avoid.

The trouble began on one of those cool September evenings the residents of Emerald Point looked forward every year as the busy tourist season wound down. Fall had finally arrived, and the little Lake George resort town where I was serving my second two-year term as mayor was taking a breather. And I was more than happy to take one with it.

I'd dug out a pile of magazines I'd been squirreling away all summer and curled up in my living room in a big recliner I loved, a reupholstered relic from my grandparents' time. I didn't even bother to turn on the television.

I was ready for peace and quiet.

The days had grown shorter, and despite upstate New York's glorious fall weather, the evening was too cold to sit on the porch for my favorite reading accompaniment—the slow, steady beat of the lake.

I'd skimmed through almost a third of the stash of articles I'd earmarked to read when an insistent banging on my back door sent me running to answer. After three years as mayor, I wasn't usually summoned for emergencies at night, but once in a while something serious warranted notifying me. My heart beat faster as I swung open the door.

The woman standing in the entranceway outside the kitchen door wasn't someone I recognized. She was probably in her forties—maybe ten years older than I— and had the wildly unkempt look of a person who'd been running for her life over rough ground. She was doubled over, clutching her mid-section and gulping loud, ragged intakes of air.

"What is it? Are you ill? How can I help you?" I knew firing off a string of questions to someone who couldn't catch her breath wasn't the best course of action, but I couldn't stop myself.

"Mayor Graham? You're Mayor Graham, aren't you?" She could barely croak out the words.

"Yes. Yes."

She steadied herself enough to explain. "I've seen you…driving by. I'm Darla Phillips. Staying with the Blakes…moved in a week ago."

I backed up and motioned her inside. "What's wrong?"

The woman, looking distraught, followed me into the kitchen.

"I need your help. I saw something, something scary.

Can you come with me? I want to show you first, and you can tell me what to do."

"Darla…"

"Darla Phillips. Please. I need your help."

"Is it Victoria? Is she ill?"

My neighbor, Victoria Blake, past seventy now, lived with her son, Arthur, a few houses away. Once the summer families were gone, the Blakes and I were among the handful of people left in the neighborhood.

"No. It's not Victoria. I've got to show you something." Darla's voice still sounded weak and shaky, but she found the strength to seize my hand in a vice-like grip and drag me toward the back door.

"Hold on. Give me a minute." I hadn't changed out of the slacks and sweater I'd worn to the office, but I'd kicked off my shoes. I motioned for her to wait as I grabbed a jacket from a hook near the door and slipped into a pair of flats I'd left there.

"Want to take my car?" I asked her

"No. No. It's easier not to." She turned on a small pocket flashlight and pulled me at an angle across my side yard and up the hill behind the house.

As I struggled after her, she cut onto the dirt road, which ran parallel to the main thoroughfare at the crest of the hill. This bumpy, deserted stretch of road wasn't my favorite place to be walking at ten o'clock on a chilly fall night. The empty cottages we passed projected a spooky, abandoned look.

When we reached the Blakes' place, the outside
lights Arthur always turned on at dusk cast welcome
beams of light around his yard.

"Is Arthur out wandering around somewhere
tonight?" I asked Darla.

Ordinarily he would have been. Arthur Blake, known
locally as the Bat Man, devoted most of his nighttime
hours to his all-consuming passion—the study of bats.

Bats were Arthur's great love, an avocation he was
distressingly quick to share whenever the opportunity
presented itself. From spring to fall, he roamed the
neighborhood at night, tallying and recording his sightings of the bats which darted through the yards and
open spaces. He'd dug a small pond in his backyard and
hung a half-dozen lights from trees and wires behind
his house. The pond and lights attracted insects, which
in turn attracted large numbers of bats. Some of the
bats, who recognized a good thing when they saw it,
then made their homes in the nesting boxes Arthur
attached to the trees on his property.

"The bat's role is far more important than most people
realize, Loren," Arthur told me several times each
summer. "A single bat can eat hundreds of insects a
night, and bats are one of the few nocturnal insect-eaters.
Birds feed mostly in the daytime, as I'm sure you
realize."

Actually, I'd never thought about it, but I took his
word for it.

"Arthur's with his mother," Darla explained as she led me past his house. "He's hired me to sit with her so he can get out, but she insisted he stay with her tonight, wouldn't let him leave."

Once Darla and I had passed Arthur's house, darkness closed in on us. When my foot banged hard against an unseen rock, my ankle twisted painfully onto its side and my loafer slid off into the dirt. As I groped along the ground for it, my patience ran out.

"Hold it, Darla. I thought you wanted me to see something close by." There was a limit to how far I'd go to be agreeable, and the pain in my ankle told me I'd reached it.

"Just a few steps more. Please. We can cut down here." Darla waited until I found my shoe, then grabbed my hand again and tugged me through an overgrown yard toward a rough stone wall.

I recognized the spot. "Wait. Is this where you're taking me? This is the foundation of the Blakes' old house. It burned down a long time ago, years before I moved here."

"You've…got to see something." Darla slid down a steep embankment and pulled me behind her as she squeezed through an opening in the stone foundation into a kind of tunnel. We inched our way down a rocky passageway in the dark until we hit what felt like a concrete slab.

A rush of cold, damp air bombarded me; the stench

of rot was overwhelming. I yanked my hand back. "Enough. I can't stay in here, Darla. I'm going to be sick."

"Please, just a few steps more. I know it smells awful, but it looks like somebody's been hanging out in here."

She fumbled around on the ground near the entrance and produced a large electric lantern. As she switched it on, I pressed my palm across my nose and mouth, trying to block out the foul odor. We were in a room of some kind, probably the cellar of the old house, now only a large, empty space with no interior walls.

As my eyes adjusted to the light, I saw that boards had been slapped up against the stone sides of the foundation to reinforce the roof. Strips of carpet formed an uneven patchwork on the dirt floor. A sagging couch, once some kind of plaid, and a faded mattress piled with tattered blankets, served as the only furnishings.

How could anyone stay in here? I felt suffocated. I couldn't breathe. "Darla, I can't stand places like this. I have to get out of here."

Darla didn't acknowledge what I'd said, but continued to pull me toward the back wall. Without warning, she swung the light upward at a jagged hole in the stone foundation.

I strained to see in the glare of the flash. Nothing at first. Then I picked out an oval shape gleaming white against the dirt and debris. I stared, forced myself to process what I was looking at. Suddenly, I saw it—a skull, a human skull, its eyes gaping holes above the grinning rictus of death.

My stomach churned. Bile, sharp and bitter, scalded my throat. I turned away, trying to catch my breath. "What...? Who...?"

When I could look back, I made out fragments of a skeleton half buried in the dirt beneath the skull. A hand reached out, beckoning, as if imploring our help. My knees buckled. I grabbed for Darla's shoulder, trying to steady myself.

I staggered over to the wall and leaned against it for support as I searched my pockets for a tissue. I was going to be sick. The stench was unbearable, but what I saw in the flashlight's beam sickened me even more. Hanging from the skeleton's exposed arm was a gold watch, clearly visible against the dark earth as a gleaming disk decorated with ornate scrollwork and glittery stones equidistant along the face. Amazingly, only one stone, the one near the six at the bottom edge, was missing.

My grandmother had owned a watch like that, a gift from her father in honor of her high school graduation. Even now, I could see it clearly in my mind—its band, an elegant gold filigree, its oval face with the old-fashioned Roman numerals set with small diamonds in several places on the dial.

She wore the watch on Sundays and special occasions, took it off when she did the washing up after dinner, laid it in a little china dish she kept for that purpose on the windowsill above the sink. I'd loved that watch. Whenever I helped with the dishes, I'd admire it lying there, twinkling in the light.

I'd never known what happened to the watch after she died, and I'd never wanted to ask my grandfather. Of course, this couldn't be the same watch. No way could my grandmother's watch have ended up in this dank basement, dangling from a skeleton's outstretched arm. That would have been impossible.

TWO

I RETREATED FARTHER from the skeleton, my body racked by dry heaves. "Darla, I've got to get outside. I can't stand being in here."

I groped blindly for the rocks on the sides of the narrow entranceway, then pulled myself up a few inches at a time until I felt a rush of fresh air across my face. I sank down on the ground.

Darla followed me up the narrow incline. "I'm sorry. I guess I should have warned you. I thought maybe I was seeing things, that it wouldn't be there if I went back. I didn't think anyone would believe I'd seen a skeleton."

I took a deep breath, steadied myself enough to speak. "I don't understand any of this. Are you saying you knew that skeleton was in there? You'd already found it? When?"

She sat next to me. "A little while ago. I didn't know what to do. I didn't want to tell Arthur. He's so emotional. I figured he'd go all to pieces."

Her explanation didn't make sense. "You found the skeleton tonight?"

She nodded.

"You went into that cellar in the dark? Darla, are you telling me the truth? Why would you have gone into that awful place in the dark?"

She covered her face with her hands. "Oh. I can see why you don't believe me. Nobody will believe me." Her voice trembled. I couldn't see her face, but I could tell she'd started to cry.

I didn't want her to fall apart. "It's okay, Darla. We'll go back to my house and have a cup of tea. We can talk there."

I grabbed hold of a big rock and pulled myself to my feet. The movement drained most of the energy I had left, but I took charge. I reached down a hand and helped her up.

This time we reversed roles. I took the lead, steering her up the steep hill. Once we reached the road, moving forward in the dark became a little easier, but not much. The night sky pressed down on us, an inverted ebony bowl, imprinted with the dark branches of evergreens and the boughs of maples and oaks heavy with dying leaves. All around us I sensed the presence of death.

We picked our way along, skirting rocks and fallen limbs. We moved faster when we reached the Blake house, relieved to find the lights still on in the backyard and the lamp in the front window spreading a wedged-shaped pattern of silver across the road.

We hit another dark stretch, but once we reached the

road's intersection with Lakeside Drive and headed
down the hill toward my house, a street lamp cast a
comforting glow all the way to my back door.

I led Darla into the kitchen and pulled out a chair for
her at the table. "Sit here and I'll make tea."

She collapsed into a chair and pillowed her head on
her arms. "A skeleton. I couldn't believe my eyes. I've
never seen anything like that before. It scared me so
when I first saw it. I thought I must be seeing things."

"Hang on. A hot drink will help, and I think I've got
some cake in here." I put the kettle on my speediest gas
burner, then dug through the lower drawer in the refrigerator for a packet of my friend Kate Donohue's
fabulous apple crisp. The perfect antidote for low blood
sugar and high nervous tension.

A few minutes later as I poured our tea, Darla lifted
her head and started to fill me in. "I'm staying with the
Blakes. I guess I said that. Helping out with Mrs. Blake.
She's a handful. She's got to be too much for Arthur.
He's not all that well himself, and he wants to work on
some records he keeps on bats."

This wasn't really what I wanted to know, but it
might be a good place to start. "Are you a relative of
theirs?"

"Distant. Arthur pays me a small salary and I…well,
frankly, I wanted a place to stay for a while and he
needed help."

"So you're Mrs. Blake's nurse?"

"No, no. I'm not a nurse. More like a companion. She's a handful."

The second time she'd used the expression. I wondered exactly what it meant. "Does she get violent? Is that what you're saying?"

"Not violent. She's just so difficult. Everything is a problem—meals, sleeping, getting her dressed even."

"And you do things for her?"

"When she lets me. She mostly wants Arthur, but he can't do it all. She's awake in the night a lot. He's exhausted."

My mind spun off in another direction. "Won't he be worried about you? Where does he think you are?"

The tears she'd been holding back started again. "I don't know. I just left. I had to get away for a little while. I can't imagine what he thinks."

"We can telephone him," I said.

"Oh no. If Mrs. Blake's asleep, the phone will wake her. I'd better get back there."

I knew better than to let that happen. "You can't leave, Darla. You've got to stay right here for now. We'll have to call the sheriff's department, let them know about the skeleton. You'll need to give the deputy the details about how you found it." I reached for the phone.

Darla's cup clattered as she dropped it into the saucer. "I can't talk to anybody tonight. Can't this wait 'til tomorrow?"

I hit the sheriff's department's number and adopted the tone I'd perfected for difficult common council members. "There's no way we can put this off until tomorrow, Darla. We have to call now."

I poured us each more tea and made another effort to get Darla to fill in the blanks. "How did you happen to go into that cellar in the first place? You said you left the Blake house earlier. Where were you headed?"

"Wait, give me a minute," she said. "I need to pull myself together if I have to talk to a deputy."

Not a bad idea for me either. I should go back over my own role in tonight's events. I'd have to make everyone understand this was Darla's discovery, not mine. I'd been involved only as a good neighbor. I'd been practically ready to go to bed, for heaven's sake, when she dragged me into this mess.

Tonight, a deputy would come to take Darla's statement, but in the morning the information would be passed on to Sheriff's Investigator Jim Thompson, a man who would be less than pleased with this turn of events.

What I needed to do was put the best possible spin on my role in the discovery of the skeleton. As I mulled over how to manage that, a conversation I'd had with Jim more than a year ago muscled its way into my consciousness. Even after all this time, I remembered exactly how it went.

"You running for reelection or not?" he'd asked me straight out one morning when he stopped by my office.

The question surprised me. "Definitely. Did you think I wouldn't?"

"Mayor, I gave up trying to figure out what you were thinking a long time ago. But what you're going to do will influence some decisions of mine, so I want to know for sure what you're planning."

"Like what decisions?" I'd asked, trying to get a read on what he was thinking.

That morning I'd detected no trace of light-hearted banter in his voice. Not that anyone expected a sheriff's investigator to have much sense of fun, but Jim and I had reached a point in our friendship when we kidded back and forth occasionally. His tone that day had been deadly serious.

And Jim, I'd realized a long time before, did deadly serious to perfection. He stood six and half feet tall with short-cropped iron-gray hair and a broad-shouldered, muscular build which, even as he approached fifty, showed no trace of fat. Although he didn't wear the sheriff's department uniform, his well-tailored dark suits, along with crisp white dress shirts and somber ties, made him an impressive figure. No rumpled, dime-novel-detective look for this guy.

In fact, Jim did deadly serious so well I resigned myself that morning to the harsh words I sensed were coming.

When he didn't respond immediately, I primed the pump. "You've obviously got something you're anxious to say to me, so go ahead. Spit it out. I can handle it."

"Okay then. I'm not suggesting you haven't accomplished some good things as mayor up here, but I'm thinking if you run again, you should confine yourself to accomplishing them as mayor, not as some sort of unpaid adjunct of the Warren County Sheriff's Department."

My mouth dropped open. My cheeks felt as if I'd leaned too close to a hot stove. *Keep it light,* I told myself. "No need for sugarcoating, Jim. Give it to me straight out."

"This isn't a joking matter, Loren. You almost got yourself killed last summer, and for that matter, the summer before too. I *am* telling you straight out. If you want backing from the law enforcement organizations around here, you should focus on your own job and let us handle ours."

Could he have made things any clearer? I'd realized on the spot I'd better take Jim's suggestion—actually his ultimatum—seriously. Since Emerald Point didn't have its own police force, we relied on the Warren County Sheriff's Department to handle law enforcement. Without their backing, I might as well concede the election on the spot.

Not only had Jim made his thinking painfully clear that morning, he'd added clout by using my first name. When he called me Loren instead of Mayor, I knew we'd crossed into uncharted territory.

Since I didn't have much choice in the matter, I capitulated fast. "Okay. Point taken. From now on, you do your job and I do mine. Is that assurance enough for you?"

"I suspect that's all I'm going to get from you right now. Just remember: I consider this an agreement, and I'm holding you to it." He uncoiled from the chair, all six feet six of him.

On that day last fall, I'd made a pact and I'd intended to keep it. Now, through no fault of my own, my new neighbor's bizarre discovery had smashed it into a million pieces.

THREE

WHILE WE WAITED in my kitchen for the arrival of a deputy, I spelled out to Darla exactly what she had to do.

"You've got to start at the beginning, Darla, and tell him one step at a time exactly how you happened to find the skeleton. There's no reason to be nervous. Just give him the facts. I can't do the talking for you. You've got to do it."

She pulled a shredded tissue out of her pocket and dabbed at her eyes. "All right. I guess I can manage it."

By then, she'd gobbled down two slices of Kate's apple crisp and drained three cups of tea. The combo would steady anybody enough for a sheriff's department Q and A—at least I thought it would.

What I hadn't counted on was her reaction to Deputy Rick Cronin when he marched through my kitchen door twenty minutes later. Even with his pink cheeks and boyish good looks, Rick, in his gray uniform and broad-brimmed gray hat, could have stepped off a sheriff's department recruiting poster.

"Mayor." He nodded at us both, removed his hat and settled himself at the kitchen table.

I made the introductions. "This is Darla Phillips, Rick. She came to me for help. I was just about to go upstairs to bed. Darla, tell Rick exactly what happened."

Rick pulled a little notebook from his pocket, jotted her name on a blank page and waited.

Darla flung her hands up to her face and burst into tears.

Exactly what I'd been afraid of. "Darla, take it easy. Tell him what you saw."

When she didn't respond, I pulled my chair up close to her and patted her arm. I couldn't tell if she was reacting to Rick's demeanor, his uniform or that damn notebook, but this was not the way I'd wanted things to go.

Darla wiped her nose, took a deep breath and sat up ramrod-straight in her chair. "I uh, uh…" was all she could get out before the tears started again.

Rick glanced over at me. "Why don't you give me the information, Mayor?"

The very thing I didn't want to happen.

"I'm sure she can do a better job of it." I aimed a sharp kick in the direction of Darla's leg, and missed.

Darla resumed crying. I offered more excuses. Finally, I had no choice but to give up and tell Rick what we'd seen.

When I finished, he stared at me as if baffled by what I'd said. "Mayor, are you telling me you followed her over there in the dark without knowing what you were going to find? Why didn't you call us before you did that?"

So I'd made a mistake. Since I couldn't come up with a good excuse, I blurted out the first thing I thought of. "Rick, maybe I was foolish to go with her, but I didn't expect anything that serious."

The deputy's boyish countenance registered not merely confusion, but disbelief. "She came after you, crying hysterically and insisting you come with her and…"

"I know. I know. I should have asked more questions," I admitted.

Before I could say more, a loud banging on my back door made us all jump. Rick stood up fast and motioned for Darla and me to stay seated. He moved quietly to the door and pulled it open it a few inches at a time.

Arthur Blake stood outside, his big fist raised to knock again. Obviously upset, he pushed past Rick into the kitchen. "Darla, what's going on? Why are you here?"

Years ago when I'd come to the lake as a child to visit my grandparents, I'd found Arthur a strange and somewhat frightening neighbor. He was oversized, a big man both in height and weight, and yet he could glide through the yards at night without making a sound.

Later, I'd learned he was sometimes referred to as slow and that he'd never held much of a job, but people in town respected him for his dedication to his mother and his intensive knowledge about the bats native to this area.

Now, without waiting for Darla to answer, he rushed over to where she sat at the kitchen table and fired off a string of questions. "Darla, what happened to you? What's wrong? Why were you gone so long?"

His agitated tone set Darla off again. She loosed a fresh torrent of tears and shook her head, unable to explain her absence. Arthur pulled out the one empty chair at the kitchen table and collapsed into it.

I went for good neighbor status by pouring both men tea and sliding plates and forks toward them so they could help themselves to Kate's apple crisp.

As Arthur dug into his apple crisp, I thought—as I always did when I saw him—that he still looked exactly as he had during my childhood visits to my grandparents. He was probably close to fifty now with a stocky build and a round face whose vertical and horizontal creases always reminded me of latitude and longitude lines and made me think of cartoon drawings of the world.

Before any of us could give him a rundown on what had happened, there was another knock on the door.

"Oh, dear. I hope Mother hasn't followed me down here." Arthur leapt to his feet and, before Rick could stop him, flung open the back door.

A middle-aged woman in an outsized black raincoat with a gray scarf wrapped around her head elbowed her way past him into the kitchen. Following close on her heels came a wild-eyed young man, heavy-set, also all in black, and sporting a mass of uncombed dark hair and an untrimmed black beard. He was the spitting image of pictures I'd seen in history books of Rasputin, the Russian holy man. My life had become totally surreal. I'd never laid eyes on either of these people before.

The woman advanced on Rick and stopped just short of shaking a finger in his face. "Officer, what's happening here? I demand to know what's wrong."

Rick pulled himself up to his full five ten, squared his shoulders and gave both newcomers his best intimidating glare. Rick might be young and rosy cheeked, but he knew how to take command. "Do you know these people, Mayor?" he asked.

I shook my head.

"Suppose you two start by telling me who you are then," he said, his pen poised over the little notebook.

Faced with Rick's assertive response, the woman did a fast job of gear-switching. "You're right, young man. We should have introduced ourselves. I'm Millicent Halstead. I've just purchased the Reynolds place on the Ridge. This man is my associate, Will Broderick. When I saw the sheriff's car pull up, I insisted he come down here with me to find out what's wrong."

Rick, still in take-charge mode, spoke in slow, deliberate tones. "I can assure you there's nothing for you to be concerned about, Mrs. Halstead. As you probably know, this is Mayor Graham—I'm here at her request.

Have you met these other neighbors, Darla Phillips and Arthur Blake? I'm Deputy Richard Cronin, Warren County Sheriff's Department."

Smooth. Rick's mother would have been proud of him.

"I have a few more questions for the mayor and Ms. Phillips," he went on. "Why don't you three go on back to your homes now and I'll make sure you get a full report tomorrow on anything pertinent. I can assure you there's nothing you should be losing sleep over."

Arthur Blake had no intention of being dismissed so easily. "I don't see why I can't bring Darla home with me now," he grumbled.

"As I told you, I have a few more questions for her. I'll make sure she gets there in half an hour," Rick said.

When Arthur began to protest again, Rick turned to me. "Mayor, if you and Ms. Phillips will excuse me for a few minutes, I'll make sure these people get back to their houses."

He was shepherding them out the door when Mrs. Halstead slipped around him and swept back to where I was standing. "Just a minute, young man. I want to invite Mayor Graham to a welcome evening I'm planning. Loren, I hope you can come to a little soiree I've scheduled for eight o'clock next Saturday. I so want you to be there."

Dumbfounded, I managed a small, non-committal smile. "Thank you."

Without another word, Mrs. Halstead turned on her heel and followed the others out.

When Rick returned ten minutes later, he was all business. "Now Mayor, you and Ms. Phillips better take me over to that cellar where you found the corpse. Coroner's not going to like being called out at this time of night, so the sooner we get on this the better."

"You think you have to call him out tonight?" I asked in surprise. "Rick, it's a skeleton. It's been there a long time. I doubt it's going any place."

"I have to take a look. I'll ask both you ladies to accompany me."

Darla and I slipped our jackets on again and followed Rick outside.

"Get in the car, please," he said as he opened the back door of his patrol car.

A good decision. My ankle still stung like crazy from my last trip.

We drove quickly over the route Darla and I had struggled along earlier. Rick used a spotlight on the side of his car to light up the terrain and, when we reached the burned-out house, trained it on the entrance to the cellar.

"Do you want me to come in with you?" I asked him.

"You don't have to, Mayor. You can wait here." He swung out of the car and picked his way down the slope and through the narrow opening.

Fine with me. I had no desire to go back into that

foul-smelling mausoleum. I huddled in the car with Darla, relieved not to have to get anywhere near that skeleton again.

It never dawned on me I could be making my second big mistake of the night.

FOUR

THE NEXT MORNING I sat at my kitchen table, guzzling down one cup of coffee after another, while I waited for the arrival of Sheriff's Investigator Jim Thompson. By this time Rick would have submitted his report on what he'd found in the cellar and Jim would already be starting his investigation.

After the deputy had finished checking out the cellar the night before, he'd decided to seal off the entrance with tape and postpone notifying the coroner until morning. At seven-thirty, I'd spotted our county coroner, Dr. Stuart Tarrington, zipping by on the dirt road in his big black Cadillac, headed for the cellar.

When Jim arrived around eight, I welcomed him with a warm smile and a hot cup of coffee. "I don't have any donuts, I'm afraid," I said in the most gracious tone I could manage at that hour, "but I've made a fresh pot of coffee and thawed some of that delicious coffee cake Kate makes. You always say how much you like it, and I had some in the freezer."

"It's going to take more than coffee cake on this one, Mayor. Just when I think you're staying out of law enforcement business like I asked you to do, you find us a body."

"Not a body, Jim, a skeleton. And while I'm not well-versed on how fast bodies decompose, I suspect it was put there long before I moved to this part of the world."

"Put there? You got some reason to think it was put there?"

His remark surprised me. "How else would it get there? Isn't that the Blakes' old house? You don't think they moved out years ago and left it in the cellar, do you?"

"Mayor, when you're involved I don't know what to think. Rick didn't understand why you went over there in the dead of night with some woman you'd never seen before."

"Jim, it was ten o'clock, not exactly the dead of night. And it was Darla Phillips, the woman who's been living with the Blakes for a couple of weeks now."

"I see. Actually, I don't see, but go on."

"When she came to my door, she was too upset to tell me what she wanted to show me. If I'd known she found a skeleton, don't you think I would have called the sheriff's department immediately?"

"Would you? You didn't secretly relish playing detective? I wouldn't be surprised if going into an abandoned cellar in the dark with a complete stranger wasn't right up your alley."

I thought I detected a hint of a smile, so I offered a

few more details. "And the cellar aspect of it was just the beginning, Jim. I wish you'd been here. Did Rick tell you? Darla Phillips couldn't stop crying long enough to tell him anything. Then Arthur Blake comes bopping in, all shook up, wondering where she's disappeared to. And he's rapidly followed by my two newest neighbors—both dressed entirely in black and crazed with curiosity about what's going on."

"That would be Mrs. Halstead and—what's the guy's name?"

"Will Broderick. The Mad Monk, I call him. He looks exactly like pictures of Rasputin. Remember that wild-eyed Russian who could stop the little czarevitch from hemorrhaging."

He gave me a sharp look. "Let's stay in this century, Mayor, not get too far off track."

"Just so you understand I was an innocent victim here."

"Rick gave me those same high points, but he didn't quite get why you felt duty-bound to rush over there in the dark yourself instead of calling the department."

Conciliation was called for. "If I admit I made a stupid decision, can I get absolution?"

Jim thought about my question before he answered. "For the time being, I suppose. No guarantees for the future."

AT A FEW MINUTES PAST ten o'clock, I dashed into the mayor's office in the small, white frame structure we called the Village Building. The early residents of Emerald Point had chosen the name years before when they decided Town Hall was too grand a designation for their quiet little community.

I wasn't surprised to find Pauline Collins, the conscientious village secretary, already seated at her desk. News traveled fast around the lake.

"I thought you might be held up, Loren, so I came in early. Hear you had a busy night," she said with a smile.

In her new navy blue suit and pink silk blouse, with her white hair brushed into an attractive halo around her head, Pauline looked ready to tackle any problem that came along, even an unidentified skeleton.

Although she'd apparently heard the high points already, I gave her the full run-down about my role in the night's events. "You know everybody who's lived around here for years, Pauline. Whose skeleton could it be?" I asked when I finished my report.

"I may be able to come up with a name for you eventually, Loren, but I'll need more time. Offhand, I can't think of anybody went missing or disappeared in recent years. No telling how long ago the death occurred, I suppose."

"Not yet anyway. What about Reggie? What's he make of it?" I said.

Pauline's husband, a French and Indian War reenactor and the town's resident expert on the area's past, was always a prime source of information on local people, living or dead. He could rattle off the names of every family in town for generations back.

"Reggie's going to ask around, says he may even scoot up to the nursing home and talk to Ethan Gregory. He's past one hundred now, you know. If Eth's having a good day, he might come out with something the rest of us don't know anything about."

"Great idea," I said. "But maybe he should hold off until Doc decides how long that skeleton's been there. He'll have to figure out how old the bones are before they can make the identification. It could turn out to be somebody from a long time ago."

Pauline chuckled at that prospect. "Reggie and the other re-enactors will flip if it turns out to be a skeleton from the French and Indian War, some poor fellow killed in one of the battles around the lake. They'll have that archeologist from Fort William Henry up here faster than scat."

"But we're a long way from the southern end of the lake, Pauline. Wasn't that where most of the battles were fought?" I said.

Pauline waggled her eyebrows, pretending to be shocked. "Better not let those guys hear you say that, Loren. You know Rogers and the Rangers did a lot of fighting all around here, harassing the French, spying on their troops moving in and out of Fort Ticonderoga."

I backed down fast. "Don't ever tell Reggie what I said."

She made a zipping motion across her lips. "Your secret's safe with me. So does Jim have any idea how the skeleton got into the cellar?"

"Even if he did, he wouldn't give out information like that right now, especially to me. But my guess is that the wall between the cistern and the cellar collapsed and the skeleton was swept along with the stones."

"And no idea why a body was in the cistern in the first place?"

"I suppose that old cistern could date way back, but nobody's speculating on how the body got in there. Fell in. Pushed in. Dumped in after death. Doc's got to come up with answers to a lot of questions first."

And if Doc determined the skeleton dated back to the French and Indian War—that would be the perfect solution as far as I was concerned. No present-day murder mystery for Emerald Point. No accusations from Jim Thompson that I was sticking my nose in sheriff's department business again. I'd be totally in the clear.

I flashed on the watch I'd seen on the skeleton's arm. I didn't think soldiers in the 1750's wore wrist watches, but what did I know?

FIVE

WHEN I DROVE HOME from the office that afternoon, I bypassed Cove Road and took the next turn off the highway toward the lake. A quick right brought me to the narrow dirt track I'd followed the night before. Doc Tarrington's car was parked outside the ruins of the house where we'd found the skeleton and two grim-faced sheriff's deputies were loading a long wooden box into the back of Olesky's hearse, the department's designated transporter of bodies.

As I watched, Doc emerged from the cellar. The coroner might have been past sixty, but he boasted the best physique of anyone in town, or for that matter of anyone on the lake. Tall and lithe, with the athletic build of a guy half his age, Doc usually radiated good health and, despite his part-time coroner duties, came across as cheerful and upbeat. But not today. Today, his face was pale with fatigue.

I rolled down my window and called to him. "Doc, you've been at that a long time. I saw you go by this morning before I left for work."

"Damn right you did. I earned my money on this

one, I can tell you." As he walked toward my car, he tugged a handkerchief out of his pocket and wiped sweat off his forehead. Looked like the hours in the dank basement had taken their toll.

"I'm about to put on a pot of coffee and make myself some lunch. Want to join me?" I asked.

"I might just do that, Mayor. Lunch breaks don't fit very well into my line of work, but when I finish up, it hits me how many hours I've gone without eating."

"I'll start the coffee. Come along when you're ready."

"Let me make sure these guys get away all right, and I'll be right behind you."

Ten minutes later my favorite Vermont-blend coffee was dripping into the carafe and the microwave was zapping a bowl of broccoli soup. By the time Doc pushed open the kitchen door, I'd riffled through the refrigerator for a selection of specialties from my good friend Kate's coffee shop and catering service—a fabulous ham salad, sliced Muenster and a stack of hearty rye bread.

He sniffed appreciatively. "You're a lifesaver, Loren. Where can I wash up?"

I pointed him toward the downstairs bathroom.

"Must have been cold in that cellar, Doc," I said when he emerged a few minutes later.

"I'm about frozen through, but some of that good food will put me on the right track." He settled himself at the kitchen table and reached for the bowl of soup I'd set out for him.

Without further comment, Doc wolfed down a humungous portion of soup, a king-sized ham salad sandwich garnished with cheese and two cups of coffee. Then he shoved back his chair and, as I'd hoped, began to repay me with information about the skeleton.

"A woman…been there twenty-five, maybe thirty years…long enough all the flesh is gone. Tests will tell us more. Maybe fell, maybe pushed into the cistern. The cover was put back on. Unless she was some kind of contortionist, she couldn't have managed that herself."

"You mean she's been in the cistern all that time?"

"I'm guessing. It looks like the cistern dried up some time before the house burned down. When the cellar wall collapsed—I'd estimate that a fairly recent event—the skeleton was carried along with the stones into the basement."

"That smell. I don't know how you could work in there."

"It was bad all right. Don't think it came from the skeleton though. The cellar was musty, and then with odors from the cistern mixed in…funny thing is it looks like somebody's been hanging out in there."

"What do you mean?"

"Old couch. Pieces of carpet on the floor. Hope it wasn't somebody hiding from the sheriff's department."

"Couldn't it have been old stuff left behind when the Blakes moved?"

"Somehow I didn't get that impression."

I shuddered. "And the skeleton? You thinking the woman was alive when she went into the cistern, Doc?"

"Hope not. Pretty bad way to go if she was. Broken bones, but they might not have happened in a fall. Too soon to tell much, but she could have been killed some place else and dumped in the cistern later."

"And you think this happened twenty-five years ago or more? You've lived around here a long time, Doc. You got any ideas who this woman could be?"

Doc pursed his lips. I could tell by his eyes he was going back in time, recalling cases where people dropped out of sight without much explanation.

I didn't want to disturb his train of thought, so I tiptoed over to the coffee maker and refilled his coffee cup.

"No idea yet, Loren. This is a puzzler. And there's a lot of ways it could play out. I'm not jumping to any conclusions. Another thing I was thinking—the person who put the cover back on that cistern maybe didn't have anything to do with her being in there."

"You mean somebody might have happened along, seen the cover off and thought he was doing a good deed?"

"Sure. Any number of possibilities. Jim's got his work cut out for him this time. He'll have to run down a lot of leads before he gets this one figured out."

Exactly. And fortunately, there was no way any of those leads could lead back to me. At least, I didn't think so at the time.

As I STOOD IN the doorway, saying goodbye to Doc, Josie Donohue slipped past me into the kitchen.

The minute I shut the door behind him, she pounced. "Hey, Lor, is it true you found a skeleton? Did you try to call me? Is there any coke?"

"Whoa. Slow down a minute." Thanks to previous experience with my seventeen-year-old friend's rapid-fire delivery, I could answer her questions in the proper sequence without wasting a breath. I nodded my head, shook it, then pointed toward the refrigerator.

Josie understood perfectly. She reached into the fridge for a can of soda and flung her slightly over-weight, seventeen-year-old body into a chair at the kitchen table.

"You saying that woman who's moved in with the Blakes dragged you to the cellar to see a skeleton? Think she's batty like Arthur?" she asked me.

"I thought we decided you weren't going to describe Arthur that way." I gave her a disapproving look as I sat down in the chair across from her.

"You decided that, Lor. Sorry. I just couldn't stop myself. Tell me how that woman got you to go over there."

"So everybody knows about this, I take it."

"Sure. What did you expect?"

"Nothing different, I guess." I presented her with a quick account of both my trips to the cellar.

"Damn. I wish you'd called me," she said when I finished.

"Believe me, if I'd known what I was going to find, I would have. In fact, I would have let you go in my place."

"Did this have anything to do with those noises you were bummed about last week? Were you hearing 'em again?"

I shook my head, a little surprised at the question. "The noises I asked you about? It never occurred to me there might be a connection. I heard them mostly on weekends, like somebody pounding on something. I doubt the skeleton was making them."

"Like I told you. Probably some new kind of noise pollution. You know how sound travels around here, especially at night. Nothing you should worry about."

Josie trying to reassure me? Had I become so needy I required help from a teenager who depended on odd clothes, a slouchy walk and a weird haircut to define herself?

After I insisted several times I'd only been curious, not worried about the noises, she switched back to her questioning. "So you'd never called on your new neighbors? You'd never met them before last night?"

"You know I'm not the type to whip up casseroles and do the welcome wagon bit."

"You don't have to be. My mother can handle that gig. She's got a couple big events coming up this week, or she'd have done it already."

And that was exactly what her mother, the hard-working owner of Kate's Catering Service, would have done. Kate never missed a chance to bring a gift of food to anyone for any occasion.

"And you don't have to worry about it either," Josie assured me. "I've got a handle on this new neighbor thing for you."

"Okay, so tell me."

"Besides that woman who dragged you over to the cellar—the one staying with the Blakes—you've got two other new people. The woman who came to your house late last night to find out what was happening is Millicent Halstead and the guy who was with her lives in her basement."

"Will Broderick," I said.

"If you say so. Don't know much about him. But Mrs. Halstead's a writer. Never wants to be called Mil or Millie, she told my mother. She does some sort of travel books especially for old people. She goes on trips herself and then writes about them, tells everybody the best places to go and the best things to do when they get there, in case they can't figure it out for themselves."

"But aren't there a lot of books like that already?" I said, amazed as I often was at the different approaches people took to the subjects they wrote about.

"She bought the big house, didn't she? Cost half a mil, they're saying in town and she didn't have to take out a mortgage."

"How do you know all this?"

"She's havin' one of the events my mother's doing next week. Mrs. H. arranged it even before she moved here. Wants it very classy. Maybe you'd get invited if you'd drag your ass up there and call on her."

"Nicely put," I said, although I realized sarcasm was lost on Josie. "I'm already invited. So there."

It wasn't much of a victory, but it was something.

SIX

LESS THAN A WEEK LATER on a warm fall evening, an hour after a fiery sun had settled behind the mountains to the west, I walked up the hill to Millicent Halstead's house and followed the slate path, lighted by white luminarias, to her front door. I knew Kate was catering the party, but I didn't have a clue who else would be there.

Cars I didn't recognize, most of them large, expensive models, already crowded both sides of the road, but there were no other guests in sight. I rang the doorbell and waited.

"Loren Graham," I said to the young man who admitted me. He was college age, decked out in a white dress shirt and black bow tie, not one of Kate's regular employees.

He responded with a lopsided grin. "Mark Palmer, greeter and bouncer—although I expect my bouncing duties to be light with this crowd. Go on in. Drinks and food to your left, conversation to your right."

The living room, which I'd seen a few times when the Watson family lived here, ran the length of the house from front to back. Oversized chairs and couches in whites and off-whites were clustered on elegant Oriental rugs. White candles in glass chimneys and lamps haloed in pink light gleamed against the rich dark wood of antique tables. A different look from the Watsons' décor with its emphasis on water skis and tennis rackets. Millicent Halstead apparently had excellent taste and the money to indulge it.

It was a perfect party setting, subdued, but elegant. A low fire burned in a white brick fireplace across from the entrance to the room and the soft music of a string quartet floated from an alcove. The guests were strangers to me, no one I recognized from Emerald Point or anywhere else on the lake.

A group of three men and two women, clustered in a corner at the far end of the room, exchanged views on an upcoming election. They weren't talking local politics I realized at once, but dissecting a New York City race. The women, who were doing most of the talking, wore the elegant ensembles many considered appropriate for cocktail parties in the city. I was glad I'd glammed up a bit in my beige silk dress and added a piece of my grandmother's antique jewelry.

When I didn't see our hostess, I headed for the buffet laid out in the dining room, hoping Kate might be serving.

A long table, draped in a heavy white damask cloth, displayed an elegant assortment of hors d'oeuvres and canapés. A second table, adorned with silver ice buckets and monogrammed glasses, served as a bar. Another young man, a clone of Mark the gatekeeper and also a stranger to me, asked my choice of drinks. As I waited for him to pour a Chardonnay, I stole a look at my fellow invitees. Not many young people, no familiar faces, definitely not a Lake George crowd.

"Make for the deck. You'll find people you know out there," a voice said in my ear. Kate Donohue, neat and trim in her black skirt, white blouse and floppy red tie, paused on her way into the living room with a tray of scrumptious-looking miniature roast beef sandwiches.

"Fabulous place, but who are these guys helping out?" I said.

"Mrs. Halstead wanted me to include them. She's used them before, I guess, and likes them. They seem okay, don't they?"

"I suppose if you like handsome young men…Don's still away, and I'm on my own tonight. Maybe we should check 'em out for later."

"Keep me posted. I'll be available." Kate hurried off, chuckling. She recognized an idle threat when she heard one.

I headed into the living room toward the open French doors leading to the deck. The guests, chatting in small groups, didn't glance in my direction. Still no sign of our hostess.

"Loren. Loren Graham."

The voice came from a dark corner at the far end of

the room. Arthur Blake, looking uncomfortable, hunkered on an ottoman much too small to support his weight. I knew the woman almost hidden in the depths of the white leather wing chair next to him was his mother, although I'd seen her only occasionally since I'd moved to the lake.

"Loren," Arthur said as he got to his feet. "I'm not sure Mother ever met you. She rarely attends evenings like this. I'd like to present you."

What I saw first was a frieze of fine, white hair, arranged in soft waves around a face amazingly untouched by the ravages of age. In contrast to Arthur's wrinkled countenance, his mother's cheeks were smooth as a child's. Only the deep-set lines around her eyes and mouth and the frailty of her body revealed she must be past seventy.

"Mother, may I present Loren Graham. I believe you know she's the mayor here in Emerald Point."

Mrs. Blake extended her hand in a languid motion that invited the most delicate of handshakes. "How do you do?"

Her hand felt boneless, as soft and pliant as a newborn baby's. When in doubt, I'd found in the political world, the wisest course of action was to follow the other person's lead. I tamped down an inclination to chatter and replied in an equally formal tone. "I'm so pleased to meet you, Mrs. Blake."

"Arthur tells me you are Ray Graham's granddaughter. I was once very fond of Ray and Carol, but time changed that, as it does so many things."

"Mother, please." Arthur, obviously embarrassed, sank back down on the ottoman.

His mother ignored his discomfort. "They were not the people I thought they were. My friendship with them turned out to be a mistake, a very serious mistake."

"Mother…" Arthur said again.

"My son is right. I'm talking about the past again, never a popular subject with you young people."

I didn't respond. After my years in Emerald Point's sometimes rough and tumble politics, I didn't expect to be surprised by anybody's reaction to me, but this woman had managed the least gracious response to an introduction I'd ever heard. Apparently, there'd been trouble between the families, but my grandparents had never mentioned it to me. I glanced over at Arthur, wondering if he would throw some light on what she was talking about, but he seemed as taken aback as I was. A good time to move on.

"Mrs. Halstead has a beautiful place here, doesn't she?" I murmured into the air as I made a tactical withdrawal through the open French doors.

The covered deck, with its sparkling green paint and white patio furniture, glowed with Millicent's signature white candles and shaded lamps. Beyond the railing, a night sky shot with a thousand pinpricks of silver light arched over the dark lake. As I approached the railing, I saw the lamp I'd left on in my own house gleaming through the trees below.

A voice in my ear startled me. "Hi. Join us."

Even in his khakis and pink shirt, the tall, gangly young man who'd detached himself from a nearby group could have won the part of Abraham Lincoln in a summer stock production. "I'm Jeff Richardson, the *Post Standard*'s recent hire. Stephanie sent me to tell you to join us."

"Loren, hi." Stephanie Colvin called out as Jeff and I approached her.

Steph, the features editor at the *Post Standard* in nearby Glens Falls, had helped me publicize a number of Emerald Point projects. A slender brunette in her thirties, she looked stunning in a splashy red print dress. Her dangling silver earrings caught the light of the candles as she set her drink on a low table to give me a hug.

"Good to see a friendly face," I said.

She winked. "And I suspect you need friends right now. The word's out you found a body. I thought you'd promised Investigator Thompson to swear off that kind of thing."

"It was a skeleton," I corrected her, "and someone else found it first. I don't think I can be held responsible."

"I believe you, but does the Sheriff's Investigator? Jim's not blaming you for the skeleton's demise, is he?"

"He hasn't so far, but with Jim, you never know."

Jeff moved closer. "I'd love to hear the details about your discovery."

"Not many to tell," I assured him. "A woman living with the Blakes apparently found the skeleton earlier in the evening. She dragged me over to the basement in the dark to verify what she'd seen."

"Why? Was there any doubt about it?"

"None at all."

Jeff signaled to a waiter circulating through the crowd with a tray of white wine. When Stephanie and I shook our heads, he picked up one for himself and set his empty on the tray. "So far, no one has been able to come up with any identification, I understand."

I nodded and made a stab at changing the subject. "What do you do at the paper, Jeff?"

Stephanie clapped his shoulder in an affectionate gesture. "Same as everybody else—as little as possible without getting fired. Sorry, Loren, but I've got to run. Get Jeff to tell you Mrs. Halstead's idea. Maybe you can give him your thoughts on that subject."

Jeff made a face at her as she walked away. "Stephanie's teasing, but our hostess has put me on the spot. She wants me to help her do a column."

"Help her how? I understood she's already a well-known author."

"She's a well-known self-promoter. The guys at the paper insist we've been invited tonight for a reason.

You're the mayor of this town, aren't you? You must be used to that kind of thing."

"I assumed I was invited because I was a neighbor."

Jeff drained his wine glass. "Don't kid yourself. Even Stephanie thinks Mrs. Halstead will come up with something she wants from all of us. Maybe not tonight, but somewhere down the road."

Apparently, these folks knew more about my new neighbor than I did. "I thought Mrs. Halstead specialized in travel books. You mean she writes for newspapers too?" I asked.

"She's written travel books up to now, but she wants to branch out by turning excerpts from her books into a column. Hopes to get into syndication eventually."

"Really?"

Jeff tightened his lips and shook his head in disgust. "We're contacts, all of us. I bet she'll discuss a project or two with somebody and write this all off as a business expense."

Not my idea of cheerful party talk. "Here I thought I was a cynic. I'm not planning on hanging around long anyway. Are you staying?"

"A friend is supposed to join me. I think I'll stay a little longer."

More power to him. I'd had enough. But if Jeff was right and Mrs. Halstead wanted something from me, she wasn't in any hurry to ask for it. I hadn't laid eyes on her all evening.

As I left the deck, I spotted our hostess for the first time standing at the far end of the living room, surrounded by clumps of guests waiting to say their goodbyes. I swung through an archway into a small den, then found a door to the front hall. Maybe I could ease myself in ahead of the crowd.

I was making my way toward the entrance when I heard my name called in a stage whisper. Will Broderick, looking even scruffier than he had the night he followed Millicent Halstead into my kitchen, hovered in a doorway, making frantic gestures in an effort to get my attention.

Now what? I wanted to pretend I hadn't seen him, but I was staring straight at him. He motioned again. Apparently, he had something important on his mind and, whatever it was he didn't intend to be put off.

SEVEN

As I walked down the hall to where Will Broderick was standing, he stepped back and signaled for me to follow him.

"Hurry, please hurry," he hissed. "I don't want her to see me. Come downstairs. I have to ask you something."

"Downstairs?" I couldn't imagine what he was talking about.

"I live down there. It's all right. It's important. I want to talk to you."

I hesitated, then gave in and followed him. He hurried ahead of me down a flight of stairs and, at the bottom, motioned me into a small living room. The furnishings bore a striking resemblance to the pieces in the elegant rooms upstairs, but they were older and shabbier. Cast-offs from Mrs. Halstead, I suspected.

"Is something wrong?" I asked.

"Sit down, Mayor. Please. I have to talk with you."

Still baffled, I dropped down on a straight chair near the door.

Will settled himself on the couch across from me.

The man needed a stylist bad, or at the very least a bossy mother or girlfriend. He also could have benefited from a good barber and a larger clothing budget. The sloppy teenager thing wasn't working for him any more, if it ever had. His black beard, streaked with gray, looked even wirier than it had the first night I saw him.

"I've been doing publicity for Millicent," he said after a deep breath, "but it's not working out. It's too much, being her employee and living in the same house. I thought you might help me find another job."

He wanted a job? I glanced past him into the small kitchen where the sink overflowed with dirty dishes. Obviously not one that required a neat appearance and domestic skills.

"What kind of work are you thinking of?" I asked him.

"I want to go to New York and work in public relations. You lived there before you moved here, someone told me. I thought you could help me." He rubbed his hands together so hard I expected to see sparks fly out.

I flashed on an image of Will Broderick, unkempt and disorganized, making the rounds of public relations firms, competing for jobs against well-groomed Ivy League types. I swallowed hard.

"New York? Do you have any idea how competitive the public relations field is? I don't mean just getting a job, but keeping it too?"

"And you don't think I could handle either one?" He lifted his chin and turned his face away with a childish pout.

He appeared so distressed I softened my tone. "Wait. I didn't mean to shoot you down. Why don't I look at your resume?"

"I don't really have one, I guess."

I swallowed again. "Then maybe you can summarize your credentials for me."

"Oh, I don't really have much in that line either. The most impressive thing I've done is work for Mrs. Halstead, and she's a second rate, small town hack."

A swallow wouldn't do justice to that statement. I allowed myself a groan. "Will, who do you think will hire you if you say things like that? If you put down both yourself and your employer, no one will take you seriously."

Will massaged his beard even harder. "You don't have any ideas for me? You're dismissing me just like that?"

"Look. It's late, and we're both tired. This is no time for serious talk. Call me at the Village Building Monday and we'll make a plan to get together." I stood up and edged toward the door.

He followed me, his expression hopeful, pathetically so. "You'll give me some ideas?"

"I'll try. But you'll definitely need a resume. Make a list of places you've worked and the dates you worked there. That will give us a starting point." I tugged open the heavy door.

"Thanks. You won't tell her you were down here talking to me, will you? She'll figure I'm up to something."

Before I could react, he'd banged the door shut behind me.

Upstairs, I found Millicent still standing near the front entrance, exchanging pleasantries with departing guests. "Do you really have to leave so early? I'm so sorry I had to take that call right in the middle of the party. We'll have to get together again soon."

The line moved slowly. When my turn came, Millicent brushed aside my prepared remarks. "Loren, I wish we'd had a chance to talk. Perhaps I can stop by your office some time when you're not busy. There's something I'd like to discuss with you."

Was this when I'd find out what she wanted from me? I could wait. My quota for unexpected exchanges in one night was already filled. I couldn't handle another right now. I nodded in the vague manner I'd perfected for long-winded common council discussions and beat a hasty retreat.

On my walk down the hill, the night air felt refreshingly cool, but when I entered the kitchen, a blast of heat hit me. I'd left windows open upstairs; it would have cooled off up there. I grabbed a glass and a bottle of white wine from the refrigerator and carried them upstairs with me, pleased to find a breeze wafting in my bedroom windows on the lake side of the house. A perfect spot to decompress.

This room was my special place, my sanctuary. When I first moved from New York into the house my grandfather left me, I'd combined two small bedrooms overlooking the water, furnished them with my favorite possessions and created the retreat I'd always dreamed of having.

Without turning on a lamp, I settled into the comfortable armchair by the window and poured myself a glass of wine. The evening had left me too wired for sleep. Mrs. Blake's unpleasant comments about my grandfather had unleashed a flood of memories I thought I'd laid to rest.

When I moved back to Emerald Point six years before, I'd been subjected to similar remarks about him, some delivered as flat-out insults; others muttered under the breath or from behind a hand. Until then, I'd never realized how many people had disliked my grandfather. To me, he was a loving presence, a little distant always, but never unkind. When I visited here, I'd spent most of my time with my grandmother. She was the important person in my life, the mother figure I needed so badly. After her funeral, my grandfather and I had stayed in touch, but I hadn't visited again.

In the last few years the digs about him had dwindled to almost nothing. Tonight, Mrs. Blake had reopened a door I'd hoped was finally closed.

Then, on the terrace when Jeff made those cracks about Mrs. Halstead's reputation as a user, I hadn't taken him too seriously. I'd even wondered if it was the drink talking. Now Will Broderick's request made me suspect Jeff was right. Why would Will be so desperate to get away from her? And what in the world could the woman want with me?

I couldn't relax. The bedroom had seemed cool at first compared to the downstairs, but I soon found myself shifting uncomfortably in my chair. I never bothered with the A.C. this late in the season, but if I opened other windows, I could create some cross ventilation. I set my glass on the floor and padded down the hall to the back bedroom.

The window there offered a picture-perfect view of the party scene. The dark bulk of Millicent's house floated above the bluff, the windows shimmering with the soft light of the candles. It was a house from another time, romantic, eerily remote. As I slid up the sash, I heard the soft melody of a Broadway show tune; the group was still playing I sank to the floor in front of the window. On the deck several couples danced slowly, pressed together like cardboard cutouts. A tall, gawky figure almost enveloped the small female shape he cuddled in his arms. Jeff must have found the woman he was waiting for.

As I started to stand up, a movement outside the house caught my attention. Someone in a dark sweat-shirt, the face hidden by a hood of some kind, emerged from the shadows and crept slowly behind the border of shrubbery that separated the manicured lawn from the rough ground at the edge of the cliff.

Had Arthur taken his mother home and come back for some late evening bat watching? I ruled out that idea quickly. The figure was nowhere near as tall and stocky as Arthur. I couldn't determine much about the person, even if it was a man or a woman, but whoever it was appeared to be staring straight down at my house.

I sat quietly, watching. The only illumination in the bedroom came from the moonlight which painted silver trapezoids on the dark wooden floor. At most, I was a shadowy form and, if I remained perfectly still, no one could be sure I was there.

The dark presence crept slowly along the cliff, staying behind the low bank of shrubs, never shifting its gaze from my house. A prickle of fear touched the back of my neck. This didn't appear to be someone from Millicent's party—a guest strolling the grounds or admiring the view of the lake. This was a malevolent presence, a stalker in the shadows, a frightening apparition, perhaps connected somehow to the skeleton in the cistern, someone who had killed once and might easily kill again.

And that presence was staring straight down at my window.

EIGHT

ORDINARILY, ON SUNDAY MORNINGS I devoted a pleasant hour to relaxing over coffee and the extra-large edition of the *Post Standard*. Ordinarily, but not after I'd spent an uneasy night speculating about the figure on the bluff and tossing restlessly from one side of the bed to the other. Even after the shadowy form had melted back into the dark yard and disappeared, even after the lights in the Halstead house had flickered out one by one, I'd been reluctant to give up my vigil at the window and go to bed.

I knew it was too soon to question Investigator Thompson on the identity of the skeleton in the cistern—but reporting a suspicious presence outside Millicent Halstead's house… Wouldn't that justify a Sunday morning phone call?

After a quick swim, I telephoned his house and started with the skeleton. "It's probably too soon for an identification of that body. That's not what I'm calling about. But it's been on my mind this morning, and I figure it must be on yours too."

"Right on both counts, Mayor." Jim kept his response curt and to the point. Not quite what I was hoping for.

"So no clues at all yet?"

"You've got that right."

I sensed he'd be quick to hang up, so I segued into the next subject fast. "Wait. I want to tell you something else. Have you met the woman who's moved in on the bluff yet—Millicent Halstead?"

When he didn't answer, I rushed on, "Well, it doesn't matter. She invited me to a party last night—big crowd, very elegant—and after I got home, I spotted something a little disturbing near her house."

"And just how did you happen to do this spotting?"

I detected an ugly note of suspicion in his voice.

"Don't jump to conclusions. I was totally innocent. My house was hot, so I went to open the window in the back bedroom. There was a guy—well, I can't swear it was a man even—a hooded figure skulking around outside Mrs. Halstead's house."

"Skulking, you say? Skulking? Did you call 911? We could have sent a car out to check."

"At first, I assumed it was one of her guests. Then I got a sense it might have something to do with the skeleton. But Jim, there'd been no point in calling 911. Whoever it was would have made tracks out of there fast the minute one of your cars pulled up."

"Well, we can't do much about it now, can we? I'll make a notation. Let me know if you see this *skulker* again."

Apparently, skulking had been too strong a word.

"Fine," I said and hung up.

LATER THAT MORNING I found out I wasn't the only one dealing with fall-out from Millicent's party. As I was pulling out of my driveway on a trip to the store, Arthur Blake, rumpled and disheveled, hurried down the hill, waving frantically.

"Loren, wait up a minute," he called.

I stopped and rolled down my window.

Arthur struggled to catch his breath. "I'm sorry if I'm holding you up, but I can't let this day go by without apologizing for the way Mother spoke to you last night. I guess you could tell I was mortified."

The truth of the matter was I'd almost forgotten Mrs. Blake's rudeness. Her unpleasant comments about my grandfather didn't seem worth worrying about after my conversations with Will Broderick and Millicent and my reaction to the figure on the bluff.

"Arthur, you don't have to apologize to me. I understand your mother's not quite herself sometimes. In fact, I was surprised to see her at the party. Has she started going out again?"

"Well, she's taking a new medication that seems to be helping her. She knew Mrs. Halstead years ago and wanted to catch up with her."

"Did they catch up?" I hadn't seen any sign of it, but maybe they'd talked before I got there.

"I'm not sure. The party might not have been the best

time for it. I'm so glad you didn't take offense, Loren.
I wanted to make sure."

"No offense taken, Arthur. You shouldn't have
worried."

ONE OF THE first lessons I'd learned when I moved to
Emerald Point six years before was the futility of taking
offense about anything.

During the summers I spent here a child, I'd formed
impressions of the town and its occupants, impressions
I came to realize were colored by my youth and lack of
knowledge. Bob Henderson, a small shop owner who
came across as unfriendly and crabby, I learned eventually, lived in constant fear that his business was about
to go under, but always found a way to help out anyone
in need. Some of the women who chatted and fussed
over me when I was with my grandmother openly
disliked my grandfather and didn't speak to him or me
if they saw us together on the street

Many families in the area were related, and Diane—
another outsider—and I often joked about the danger
of finding fault with anyone since the person could well
be related to someone in the group you were talking
with.

All of which made it surprising that I'd been elected
mayor the first time I ran for any kind of office. I hadn't
expected it to happen, and from the announcement on
election night in November that I was the new mayor

until my swearing in on the first of January, I'd tortured myself on a daily basis that I was making a huge mistake.

New Year's Day was traditionally the time for the mayor and the members of the Common Council to be sworn in at a ceremony in the Council's chambers, located upstairs over the mayor's office in the Village Building. I'd been shocked that year at the heavy layer of dust along the baseboards, the appalling collection of stains on the threadbare carpet, the mismatched furniture and the poorly planned ceremony arranged by the outgoing administration.

Don had been in the audience that day, along with Diane and Kate, all of them primed to offer moral support and applause at regular intervals. Pauline and Reggie and some of their friends had turned up. Reggie had even foregone his French and Indian War uniform to appear in a sport coat and tie. A small, but loyal turnout.

The second time I sat on the dais with the Common Council members and listened to the Pledge of Allegiance delivered by a troop of local Boy Scouts, more than a hundred people crowded into the meeting room. The room sparkled after a two day cleaning spree I'd arranged with a local janitorial service and, as I welcomed the new members of the Council and spoke about the accomplishments the community had made during the last two years, I allowed myself to relax and feel as if I finally belonged.

But there was always more work to be done.

The Monday after Millicent's party I arrived at the office early, determined to make a dent in the bottomless pile of reports Emerald Point was required to file with the state. I'd finished one and was about to tackle the next when I heard a light tapping on the door casing.

Millicent Halstead poked her head into the office. "Good morning, Mayor. Your secretary has apparently stepped out. I'm hoping you can spare me a few minutes."

I jumped up and moved around the desk to extend my hand. I didn't explain that Pauline and I split the day, that I usually didn't have a secretary on hand during the morning. "Come in, Millicent. What can I do for you?"

"I'm so glad you're calling me Millicent. Dispense with formality, I always say. I'll sit a minute, if you're sure you can spare the time. I want to give you a copy of my first book and run an idea by you."

I accepted the bright red book she handed me. Rather than go back behind my desk, I sat down in a chair next to her, an arrangement which seemed to put visitors at ease. Not that Millicent appeared to be anything but completely at ease.

"*Lakeside Ramblings.* You wrote this? Is it about Lake George?" I examined the aerial photograph of the lake on the cover, then turned the book over to read the blurbs on the back. Several well-known residents of the region had offered lavish praise.

"I'll be promoting it all around the lake this summer, along with my new book, *Travels by Myself*. And I've had a fabulous idea about what to do with my proceeds."

She paused, giving me a chance to ask the question. So I asked it. "An idea?"

"Yes, Loren. Do you know I lived here years ago?"

"Really? I had no idea." Was that when Victoria Blake had known her? I wasn't sure why, but I'd assumed they met some place else.

She nodded. "Almost thirty years ago. It doesn't seem possible it's been that long."

"You lived here in Emerald Point?" Why hadn't the town been buzzing with that piece of news?

"As a matter of fact, the house I just bought is the house I lived in. My attorney approached the Watsons some time ago to see if they'd be interested in selling. It took time and a little—let's say horse trading—and they finally agreed to sell it to me at a reasonable price."

She'd lived here before? And in my grandparents' neighborhood? I racked my brain, trying to remember if they'd ever mentioned Millicent or a Halstead family. I'd spent most of my childhood summers only a short distance down the hill from her house. Could she have been living here then?

"Did you know my grandparents?" I asked her.

"I knew who they were, of course, but we didn't neighbor much."

"We? You had family here too?"

"I lived here with my husband at the time, Carl Durocher. I expect you recognize the name?"

"Carl Durocher? You were married to Carl Durocher?"

When I realized I sounded as if I couldn't imagine her married to someone so famous, I made a fast course correction. "I had no idea. I studied his poetry in a college lit class I took. He has such a wonderful reputation."

"Much deserved, as least as far as his work is concerned. His essays are taught in many colleges today and, of course, his poetry too. He's considered a twentieth century icon in both disciplines, you know. Unfortunately Carl's personal life wasn't always commensurate with his talent."

I figured a sympathetic look would elicit an explanation of that statement, if she wanted to say more. It did.

"I was very young when we were married. He wanted a quiet place to work and someone to free him from every annoyance—meal preparation, manuscript typing, dealing with people who made inroads on his time—tradesmen, editors, bill collectors. And of course, he had insatiable sexual needs. He saw my constant availability as essential if he was to do his best work."

Oops. How much did I want to hear on that topic?

I cast around for a way to redirect the conversation. "Did the two of you live here for a long time?"

"Only about a year, actually. Carl was offered a writer-in-residence position at a prestigious New England college. He decided that was what he wanted, so we moved. Enough about him. It's been a long time since the divorce, but it still distresses me to talk about him."

I offered another sympathetic look and attempted to shift gears. "You mentioned an idea you had, Millicent."

"Oh yes. I've been told Emerald Point is still recovering from serious storm damage—a tornado, was it?—the summer before last. I think we all know from the debacle in New Orleans how long it takes for an area to come back. Not that I'm implying you suffered that much devastation, but for a small town with limited resources to draw on, the damage you sustained must have been a matter of serious concern."

I felt as if I'd jumped on a merry-go-round, but I hung on gamely.

"Here's my idea, Loren. I mentioned that I will be promoting my new book around here. Of course, fall isn't the best time to do it, but it wasn't ready for me to take advantage of the summer season. I'm suggesting you join me in that effort, attend the club meetings and book talks I arrange, assist me by being a second pair of eyes and hands. I'm sure you know in your line of work how important it can be to have someone, shall we say, watch your back. You'll do that for me and, in return, I will turn over all the profits from my sales this fall to the town for your community projects. All the profits. I'm hoping that will be a sizeable amount."

I stammered out the first thing I thought of. "But I have a regular schedule as mayor."

"Not a problem. Most of my talks will take place evenings and weekends, times when I doubt you are required to be in your office. And when you're tied up with a meeting or something, I'm sure with a little advanced planning we can work it out."

Since I was stumped for an answer, I tried the truth. "Millicent, I don't know what to say."

"Oh my dear, it's a very generous offer, if I do say so myself. And it will mean help for your town. All you have to do is say yes."

So I did.

NINE

A WEEK LATER Millicent called to tell me she'd made arrangements for her debut appearance at a luncheon at the Lake George Club.

The club, located only a few miles from Emerald Point, was a half-timbered, stucco Victorian with adjoining tennis courts and a grid of docks. Built in the early 1900's to promote sports and sociability among the summer families, the club had escaped the commercialization so rampant along other sections of the lakeshore.

The building featured massive stone arches on the lake side, a wide terrace where members dined by candlelight on summer evenings and a magnificent view of the changing colors on the mountains across the lake. In short, a perfect venue in which to launch her sales efforts.

The morning of the luncheon when Millicent picked me up in her black Cadillac, she seemed totally at ease. "I've remembered everything, I think. I've brought more books than we can possibly sell and a variety of promotional materials to set out on the tables."

"Your new book should lead to an interesting discussion." I held up a copy of *Travels by Myself,* the thin, red volume she'd dropped off at my office a few days before. The book's message was simple and direct: Any woman could travel alone successfully if she planned carefully and made sensible decisions.

When we arrived at the Lake George Club shortly after eleven that morning, Millicent found a parking place close to the entrance. "Let's go right in. I'm sure someone will bring the boxes of books in for us," she said.

Once inside, she greeted the manager, the maitre d' and several of the staff, and made sure we were all on a first-name basis. "As you probably know, Loren is our mayor in Emerald Point. I'm so pleased she's agreed to be here with me today."

The introductions out of the way, Millicent pulled the maitre d' aside to confirm the arrangements she'd made over the phone. "I'm disappointed we're not using the terrace, but I totally understand. I realize it would be much too chilly out there," she said.

"Most of our parties find this space very accept-able," the maitre d' assured her. "The founders named this area the Assembly Room. It's a perfect designation, don't you think?"

The tables were already set for the luncheon. Crystal wine and water glasses glistened against sparkling white tablecloths. The silverware gleamed in the sunlight slanting in from the wide windows on the lake side of the building. Every table featured a bouquet of fall flowers.

As Millicent had predicted, two young waiters materialized and offered to help. She dispatched them to bring in the boxes of books from her car and pointed out a long table in the corner of the room that she'd designated for book sales.

When they returned with the books, she turned to me. "Loren, rather than get in each other's way, I think it best for you to handle all details of the selling. I'll stand near the doorway and greet the guests."

Fortunately, I'd seen how vendors at our annual Third of July Festival set up their stalls. I unpacked the boxes and arranged the books in stacks on the long table, one displaying the front and the other, showing the back cover with Millicent's photo clearly visible. I set out posters featuring accolades for the book and a small, discreet sign giving the price. Then I unpacked the cash box and tucked it out of sight behind one of the posters.

Millicent, her face flushed with excitement, stood near the entrance welcoming early arrivals. Her moss green suit provided a perfect accent to her dark eyes and the carefully styled black hair, accented with only a few streaks of gray. The look was elegant, but understated, an excellent choice for a fall luncheon.

Thirty years ago Millicent had lived here as a young wife, catering to a difficult husband. How old was she now, I wondered. Fifty? Fifty-five? Whatever life had been like for her in those days, she'd managed to age well. Her skin was flawless, beautifully made up. Her hands—always a giveaway for age—were soft and smooth, the nails perfectly shaped and polished.

The guests, the majority of them women Millicent's age or older, wore elegant suits or embroidered sweaters in rich autumn shades. This luncheon was probably the first post-summer event for most of them, and the arrival of cooler weather always provided an occasion to dress up in this part of the world.

I recognized most of the women easily. Some I'd met many times at other Emerald Point activities. Others I knew by name. One group, made up of both men and women, were strangers to me, possibly friends of Millicent's from wherever she'd lived before she moved here.

After she'd exchanged a few words with each of her guests in turn, Millicent pointed them toward my table. Many of them lingered near her, anxious to engage her in conversation for as long as possible. Finally, the crowd began to trickle across the room toward me, the women digging into their pocketbooks as they prepared to make their purchases.

"Will I be able to get Millicent to autograph this?" several of them asked.

"Definitely," I assured them. "She's signed some already, and it you want something more personal, she'll do it after her talk."

Sales were brisk. Millicent had set the price of the

book at $20, sales tax included, a wise decision I realized when I seldom needed to make change.

The next hour passed swiftly. The waiters circulated through the room, serving wines and salads, then wheeled in heated carts with the luncheons. At a signal from the maitre d', they began uncovering the plates with appropriate flourishes and setting them in front of the guests.

As always when food was served, the noise level in the room dropped. The women still waiting to buy books made their purchases quickly and hurried off to join friends at their tables.

Although Millicent had saved a place for me next to her, I decided to skip the meal and take advantage of the lull to run a quick total of the checks and bills. My first tally—somewhere over $1200.

As soon as coffee and a fabulous-looking fruit torte had been served, Martha Eggleston, always in the forefront of Emerald Point cultural activities, rose to introduce the speaker. She didn't make any references to Millicent's personal life, to her stay at the lake years before or even to her recent return. Instead, she limited her remarks to a brief welcome and a number of enthusiastic comments about the book— some of the same accolades which appeared on the poster at my table.

As Millicent was beginning her talk, I heard a strange hiss coming from a service doorway behind me. I turned to see Will Broderick, looking even more unkempt than he had the other times I'd seen him, motioning to me from the hall.

I offered a smile and a half wave, but Will wasn't satisfied. He gestured emphatically and mouthed the words, "Come out."

I frowned and shook my head.

"Yes. I've got to talk to you."

This time he spoke loudly enough that two women at a nearby table turned in his direction.

Before he could disturb anyone else, I signaled him to give me a minute, then closed the strong box and tucked it under my arm. I slid my chair back as quietly as possible and tiptoed out into the hall.

"Will, what are you thinking of?" I whispered.

"I've got to talk to you," he insisted. "I'll only take a minute. You can go right back."

A number of worst-case-scenarios involving people I cared about tumbled through my mind. An accident, an injury, unexpected death? "What's wrong?"

"Come over here where she can't see me." Will tugged me by the arm into a small service bar. As he leaned close to me, I got a strong whiff of alcohol on his breath. This was obviously not his first visit.

"Will…for heaven's sake, tell me what's wrong."

"Have a drink first." He signaled to one of the waiters who slipped behind the bar.

To my surprise the young man, drew a glass of beer

and slid it toward Will, then glanced expectantly at me. "Something for you?"

I shook my head and he hurried off.

Will took several gulps of beer and settled back on one of the bar stools. "Sit down a minute. I want to know how the charming Mrs. Halstead, the well-known author and lecturer, is doing right now. How's she handling things?"

"Why don't I go find out?" I snapped and started away.

"Wait. Do you know they identified that skeleton you found? Turns out it's a buddy of Mrs. H. from the old days, except nobody's made that connection yet. I thought she might be too upset to appear this afternoon."

"Will, what are you saying? How do you know this?"

"She blurted it out to me this morning after she heard the report on the radio. Two minutes later, she swore me to secrecy, said she's not letting on to anyone else."

"The radio? Is that how she found out?"

"Every radio station has the story, the television channels too. Bet she didn't turn her car radio on coming up here."

"You think she's not going to acknowledge she knew her?" I asked.

"Not yet anyway. Playing it cool, not letting on."

"But that's terrible for her, having to come here today with that on her mind."

Will showed no sympathy. "Serves her right, I say.

She hired you for my job, you know. You must have realized that. I'm the one supposed to sell books for her at these things. Now she's dumped me."

"Will, you told her you were going to quit."

"I told her that, but she knew I didn't mean it." His words slurred together.

"But, if you said you were quitting…"

"I tell her that all the time. You'll find out what she's really like. You're her good buddy right now, but you wait." He swayed back and forth on the barstool.

"I don't know what you're talking about."

"Wait 'til she decides to walk all over you. You have to keep a balance, the yin and yang, don't you know?" He struggled to enunciate his words, but they were almost unintelligible.

From somewhere in my past, I called back my sternest New York City tone of voice. "Will, go sit in that booth over there and close your eyes. Sleep for a while. You can't drive, but you can go home with us later. And don't make a scene. You'll never get things straightened out with Millicent if you spoil her talk." I grabbed his arm and tugged him off the stool.

I expected him to resist, but to my surprise he let me guide him across the room. I gestured at a booth; he lowered himself into it and dropped his head on his arms. Almost immediately, his eyes drifted shut.

I watched him for a few minutes until I thought sure he'd fallen asleep, then tiptoed back to my seat.

By this time, Millicent was wrapping up her talk, summarizing the suggestions she'd made for women traveling alone. Most of them could be summed up in two phrases—use common sense and plan carefully—but the audience leaned forward in their seats, as if hanging on her every word. She left the podium to generous applause.

As Millicent embarked on the anticipated book signings, I hurried back to the sales table where women who hadn't purchased books earlier were milling around, waiting for another chance. Millicent remained at the front of the room, inscribing personal notes for the fans who surrounded her and held out their books to be signed.

When my selling duties were done, I picked up the strong box and slipped back down the hall to check on Will. To my relief, he was still huddled in the booth exactly as I'd left him, his head pillowed on his arms.

I'd stopped at the ladies' room off the bar and was heading back to the Assembly Room when I heard Millicent, speaking softly, just beyond a turn in the hall. "But Julia, all that happened so many years ago."

I couldn't see the woman she was talking to, but I heard her response. Her voice whined like an electric drill. "You think enough years have gone by for me to forget? I'll always remember what you did, what you all did. I can't believe you had the nerve to come back here."

Millicent's voice became even softer, more placating. "Julia, I so hoped we could be friends again."

The woman's voice was louder now. "Friends? You thought I could be your friend? You must still be using, using something even stronger than you did in the old days."

"Julia, a lot has happened since the last time I saw you. And now, if they're right about that skeleton... aren't things bad enough? Why do you want to make them worse?" The pleading note in Millicent's voice surprised me.

The voice escalated to a shriek. "Worse? You're the one making things worse. Why did you come back here? To smash something else to pieces? This time you won't get away with it."

I pressed back against the wall as Millicent rushed past me toward the Assembly Room. She'd discarded the persona of the gracious author. Her face, now streaked with tears, was twisted into an ugly mask.

Julia's threats pursued her down the hall. "You won't get away with it, I tell you. Everyone will find out."

TEN

As Millicent disappeared into the Assembly Room, a flash of lightning lit up the hall windows. In almost the same moment, a horrendous clap of thunder reverberated through the building.

Before I could move, the woman I assumed must be Julia-white-haired, fragile looking, visibly distraught-came stumbling toward me. As she reached me, she pitched to the side, almost losing her balance in her haste.

"Wait. Are you all right? Can I help you?" I put out a hand to steady her.

"No. No. I'm all right. I've got to get out of here." She staggered again and banged into the wall.

"Let me take your arm. I'm Loren Graham…from Emerald Point. You're Julia…?"

"Prescott. Julia Prescott."

"Do you live nearby, Julia?"

The woman's head bobbed nervously. She raised a wizened hand to her face, as if she could stop her head from shaking. "I'm visiting here, and I've got to leave. I'm riding with someone."

"Are you sure you're all right?"

"Yes. I've got to go." She whirled around and lurched away from me.

I followed her into the Assembly Room, now a scene of mass confusion. The women were all on their feet, crowding through the exits to the parking lot. Above the choppy surface of the lake, jagged streaks of lightning ripped through a sky gone black as night. Another crash of thunder brought startled gasps from those still inside.

I watched Julia Prescott push her way through the crowd, her face bleached as white as the crumpled linen on the tables. A woman who looked enough like her to be her sister detached herself from the group she was with to grab her hand and pull her toward the door.

Once I was sure someone was looking out for Julia, I rushed back to the bar to Will. "Wake up. We're going to get a bad storm. I'm sure Millicent will give you a ride, but you have to hurry."

Will sobered up enough to follow me and help pack up the remaining books. He squatted next to the table where I'd been selling them, tumbling them into the boxes. His big hands moved quickly as he jammed the flaps of the boxes down and interlocked them.

"I'll help you take them to the car," he said.

Millicent walked over to us but ignored Will, even turned her face away as she picked up the money box and posters and stalked off toward the exit. Will and I, each lugging a box of books, followed her. By the time we'd shoved the boxes into the trunk and Will had climbed into the back seat, the first torrents of rain had swept off the lake.

"Want me to drive, Millicent? It's late in the season for a storm like this, but it looks like it's going to be a bad one," I said.

She gave me a disbelieving look. "Of course not. Get in."

I hadn't had time to fasten my seat belt when she started the car and wheeled out of the parking lot. The wipers on the Mercedes slammed back and forth in a fruitless effort to clear the windshield.

I would have liked to see Millicent pull off the road and wait out the worst of the downpour the way many other cars were doing, but we slogged on. Will and I exchanged looks as we careened down the hill into Emerald Point. We raced through the business district as if the demons of Hell were hot on our heels. The streets were deserted except for a few shoppers who huddled in the doorways of stores, waiting for a chance to dash to their cars.

As Millicent swung into my driveway, she said, "Don't worry about the books. They can be left in the car for now."

I didn't tell her I hadn't been at all worried about the books—that I'd been more concerned about skidding to my death on the slippery pavement. But since I thought the day should end on a positive note, I said, "You had a good response today. Didn't you think so?"

"Yes. I thought it went very well. I'll be in touch," she said.

I pushed open the car door and made a dash for the house. Millicent was gone before I reached it.

As I unlocked my kitchen door, I heard the jangle of the phone. My machine clicked on.

"Mayor, call me when you get in." Jim Thompson's no-nonsense voice, leaving a message.

I grabbed the receiver and caught him before he hung up. "Jim, I just came in the door. Hang on while I turn off the machine. What is it?"

"We got an I.D. on that body you found. Doc's done some fast work for us. Preliminary findings only, understand."

No sense admitting I knew the area radio and television stations had already announced the findings. "And…"

"Skeleton identified as a woman named Roberta Canfield. Not much more than twenty when she died, if that. May have been from the Albany area. We'll be checking the colleges there, requesting records. Probably won't know much more until we pin down a few more details. Best guess right now is that she might have come up to the lake for a summer job."

I knew Jim well enough now to read between the lines. "You found something to indicate she was a college student?"

"Class ring. On a chain. Looks like she might have

worn it around her neck. Large size, so it may have been a boyfriend's ring."

"And the watch? I saw a watch, on her arm, didn't I?"

"Doc hasn't mentioned a watch to me."

"Shouldn't there be a missing person's report on her?"

"Can't tell yet. People who knew her may have thought she just took off. You know how it is around here in tourist season. Kids come for a job. If things don't work out, they decide to leave. Some don't even bother to give notice."

"So what does Doc think happened to her?"

"You know she'd been in that cistern for a while. As long as twenty-five years or more."

"Why would the walls collapse after all this time?"

"I've got a pretty good suspicion how that happened, Mayor, and I suspect you do too."

"And just how would I know that?" I said.

"Maybe your young friend Josie Donohue can fill in some of those blanks for you. Why don't you ask her?"

ELEVEN

Ask Josie Donohue?

I might not have children of my own, but I knew enough about adolescents to realize that early on a Saturday evening was no time to ask a high school student with a newly acquired social life about anything. By now, Josie would have put the finishing touches on the shabby chic look she cultivated for weekend partying, made a series of phone calls to check out the scheduled action and escalated her ongoing disagreements with her mother to storming-out-the-door status. If by some remote chance she was willing to take time to answer my questions, her responses would be monosyllabic at best.

But Josie wasn't the only person who could provide me with information, and I had many questions. I made a quick phone call to my friend Diane Anderson and she agreed to meet me at Mario's Restaurant at six-thirty.

Mario's, a cheerful, old-fashioned pizzeria with a bar near the front entrance and booths and tables in back, satisfied the needs of locals and visitors alike. The present owner, the third generation Mario to run the place, offered the same authentic Italian menu in the same casual atmosphere which had spelled success for his father and grandfather. And year after year, he kept his loyal clientele coming back when other restaurants in town prospered for a time, then faded into oblivion.

Saturday night meant a crowd. I arrived a little after six and grabbed one of the last empty booths. By the time Diane came in, I'd ordered my favorite Chardonnay and an antipasto which I hoped would stave off the hunger pangs gnawing at me.

"Sorry I couldn't wait," I told her when she slipped into the seat across from me a short time later. "I've ordered enough for both of us, so dig in."

"I thought this was the day you were selling books at Mrs. Halstead's luncheon. Don't tell me she didn't feed you."

"Strictly my own fault. Her guests bought like there was no tomorrow. I took time to reorganize while they were eating lunch."

"Her sales went well then? How did she treat you?"

Diane's question surprised me. "All right. Why do you ask?"

"Rumor has it that Carl Durocher treated her like an unpaid servant. Sometimes people like a chance at payback."

"I didn't get any sense of that."

As we shared the antipasto, Diane persisted with the questioning. "Do you think any of the people in her audience knew her before? I understand she and Carl had quite the rep around here."

"I did overhear one exchange she had with a woman I didn't recognize. Some very bad blood between the two of them apparently. So what have you heard?"

Diane nibbled on a piece of salami. "You know she once lived here with Durocher in the same house she owns now, at least for a short time anyway."

"She told me. But Pauline doesn't remember her. That's unusual. Pauline is usually right on top of that sort of thing."

"Millicent's name may have been different then. I spent the afternoon in the center library checking in an order of new books. I thought I could do a little research for you. Hang on, let's order our pizza." She signaled to Liz Wentworth who was waiting tables in our section.

Even though the restaurant was full by this time, Liz delayed taking our order to give us a full account of the new puppy she and her husband had bought that afternoon. I was bursting with curiosity by the time we decided on our pizza toppings and Liz hurried off to another table.

"Diane, what kind of research? Tell me."

"Well, first I overheard some snide remarks from a couple of our patrons. Mostly Millicent's name and whispered comments. Then Candace Parker decided to check out the *Post Standard* microfilm. Thought she could zero in on the dates Millicent lived here at the lake."

Leave it to Candace. She thrived on gossip. "Did she? Find anything, I mean?"

"No. But I thought she gave up too easily. After she left, I took the microfilm she was using and turned up some references she missed. I copied a few page numbers for you." She opened her large leather pocketbook and pulled out a folded paper containing dates and page numbers.

"You mean I can find these pages on your microfilm rolls?"

"And more, I expect, if you keep searching. These are from the *Post Standard,* but there was a small local paper at the time called *Emerald Pointers.*"

"I've heard it mentioned, but I don't think I ever saw one," I said.

"Last spring when I was organizing donations people made to the library, I stumbled across a couple of rolls of it on microfilm. It was a nasty little scandal sheet about happenings around the lake, especially here in town."

"And…?"

"Loren, I only skimmed through a couple of issues, and that was months ago. I don't remember any specifics."

Now she really had my attention. "I'm supposed to eat pizza with this on my mind? At least give me a hint about what Candace and her friends were looking for."

"Wild parties, wife swapping, or whatever you call it when everyone in the swap isn't married. Other improper liaisons. You can probably guess what kind."

I looked blank and shook my head.

"Professor and student, or I should say students, plural."

"Carl Durocher? With his reputation? I thought he was the grand old man of poetry."

"He wasn't a grand old man then, remember. Probably in his early forties and exposed every day to nubile young women. He wouldn't be the first prof to offer an A for a lay."

"You think?" My image of Carl Durocher did a tailspin.

Diane smiled at my reaction. "Maybe you need to check some of this for yourself. I'll be working at the center again tomorrow afternoon if you want to find out more."

Of course, I wanted to find out more, but I didn't want to wait. "Why can't we go tonight? It's not that late."

"I've got to beg off tonight. Johnny has midterms this week, and I've already missed one call from him. He's going to phone again around ten, so I want to be there."

I understood. Since Diane's divorce from John Anderson a few years before, she considered her son her top priority. Now in his second year at George-town, the boy earned super grades and kept in close touch with both his parents.

"Diane, would you mind if I went by myself?" I asked her.

I reached deep into my pocketbook for my ring of keys and held up the one which opened the center's front door. Even though Diane assumed responsibility for the center's day-to-day operations, I still had keys to the building.

She scowled at me over a slice of pizza. "I don't think you should go up there by yourself tonight, Loren. There won't be anyone around. Why not wait 'til tomorrow?"

Not what I wanted to hear. "I expect Millicent to call me tomorrow. If I'm going to find out anything to make me bow out of our arrangement, I'd like to know it before I talk with her."

"I suppose I'll never convince you to wait," she conceded. "Your key will let you into the main room. The microfilm readers are in the little glassed-off space to the left, and the key to that room is in my desk drawer. There's a tag with a big red M attached to it."

"Easy enough," I said.

She made one final attempt to dissuade me. "I still wish you'd hold off until tomorrow."

"You're such a worry-wart, Diane. We have night meetings there all the time. Why would tonight be any different?"

But of course it was.

TWELVE

THE BUILDING WE'D CONVERTED into our community center nestled in a grove of trees on the grounds of the Emerald Point Inn. At one time it had served as a recreation hall for the Inn's guests, but its distance from the main building had limited its usefulness. Two years before, John Roberts, who owned the Inn, had agreed in a burst of generosity to lease it to the town.

As I pulled into the parking area ten minutes after I left Diane, I had to admit the center looked a little spooky at night. Its windows yawned dark and empty and the absence of street lamps along this section of the road added to the gloom. The few houses nearby appeared deserted.

When I slid my key into the lock on the front door, I steeled myself not to think about the night I'd found a body in the Rogers' Rangers display case, but of course, the memory came rushing back. I flicked the light switch in the entrance hall and moved quickly into the main room before I could change my mind and high tail it back to my car. I stole a quick look at the display case and made sure Rogers and his Rangers were all present and accounted for, with no lifeless body added to the mix.

I didn't waste time, just fished the key out of Diane's desk drawer as instructed and unlocked the glassed-in area where the microfilm readers huddled together in a tight little circle. The enclosure was bright, too bright, under the glare of the ceiling lights. Beyond the glass, the main room lay shrouded in shadow.

I quickly realized Diane's assessment of Candace's research skills had been right on target. She hadn't searched carefully enough. I needed only a couple of minutes to find the references to Carl Durocher Diane had jotted down-a short account of his move to the lake thirty years before, a real estate listing about his purchase of the house near my grandparents, then a longer article about the publication of his first book of poetry at the end of that summer. *Wanderings,* the book was called, and the lines quoted showcased his talent.

The review accompanying the article ranked Durocher's tributes to nature on a par with Wordsworth's and included one stanza from a short, but touching love poem. I caught a wisp of erotica, no more than a hint. The *Post Standard* wouldn't chance offending its readers with anything more than that.

I checked out the rest of the index, looking for Carl Durocher's name, then searched for subject headings like Emerald Point and Lake George Poets, but there was nothing more. No references to Millicent or the couple's decision to leave the lake.

Outside the wind came up, rattling the windows in their frames. I heard the old furnace kick on, a sure sign the temperature was dropping. The building groaned and creaked with noises I couldn't identify.

Disappointed, I rewound the reel I'd been using and slipped it back into its box. As I replaced it on the shelf, I cast one last look at the other microfilm boxes. Tucked in the corner, slightly removed from the rest of the collection, I caught a glimpse of two dilapidated boxes I hadn't noticed before. I moved closer. The words, *Emerald Pointers,* were stamped across them. If Diane hadn't clued me in on the name, I wouldn't have realized what I was seeing.

I sat back down at the reader and gently shook one of the reels out of its box. The film was so soft and fragile it seemed ready to disintegrate. I slid the reel carefully onto the holder and threaded the battered end of the film through the machine. I eased the film onto the pick-up reel and turned the crank slowly, half expecting the microfilm to tear as it wound through.

I didn't have to move it far. At the very beginning of the reel the editors, or whoever had transferred the print copies to microfilm, had provided an index. A quick slide to the D's and I found the name I was looking for: Durocher, Carl, followed by a long series of page numbers.

I advanced the film carefully from one article to the next. Diane had been right: *Emerald Pointers* could definitely be classed as a scandal sheet. In fact, its celebrity trashing rivaled that in the papers on today's supermarket racks. And Carl Durocher had been a prime target.

One after another I skimmed through the articles Candace had hoped to find—reports of wild parties, drunken excursions on the lake at night, hushed-up boating accidents, along with accounts of nude bathing and implications of wife swapping. I wondered how the paper had managed to escape lawsuits. But then, maybe it hadn't. Maybe that was why there were so few issues.

The parties described in the articles were attended by both fellow faculty members and students. "Swing is the word," the author of one piece declared, and "I don't mean Benny Goodwin. We're talking *sexcapades* here, gang."

At first I was relieved to find no references to Millicent. Then a few pages later, I stumbled on a description of her as "the hostess with the mostest, and in more ways than one."

I was hooked; I couldn't quit. For the next half hour, I heard only the soft whirl of the machine and the scratching of my pen as I feverishly jotted down notes on what I was finding. I would have liked to borrow the reels to use on the reader in the Village Building, but it didn't seem right to take them out of the center without Diane's okay.

The handle tightened, became harder to turn. The

reel squeaked. I bent my head close to the film and eased it along with my fingers. I was concentrating so hard I didn't notice the escalating sounds of the storm until a gust of wind slammed against the window behind me. The glass clattered as if a powerful hand had shaken it.

I whirled around in time to see a shadow sweep across the window. Had someone or something run past outside? I couldn't be sure. As I stared out into the darkness, rain pelted the glass, first in scattered drops, then as a sudden downpour which buffeted the windows with such force I thought someone was knocking to get in.

The room grew colder. A cacophony of sounds assailed me from both outside and inside the center. The wind wailed, died down, then roared back with a vengeance. The branches of the evergreens creaked as they rubbed together. Inside the old building, rattles I couldn't identify grew more menacing. The drapes at the windows trembled, powerless before the force of the drafts blowing through the casements.

Beyond the microfilm enclosure, in the main part of the center, something heavy tumbled off a shelf and crashed to the floor. My heart skipped a beat. The sweep of cold air hitting my feet made me suspect a door or window had been blown open by the force of the wind.

Suddenly, with no warning, the power went off. Fade to black—wasn't that what they called it in film making? But there was no fading; the lights simply vanished without a flicker. The microfilm reader gave a small hiccup as its screen darkened. I waited. A downpour like this couldn't last. The lights would come right back on, wouldn't they?

In the dark, the sounds I'd been hearing grew louder, more menacing. I'd had enough. I got to my feet and fumbled behind me for my jacket. I patted the fabric, relieved to feel the center keys and my car keys still in the pockets. I didn't dare try to rewind the film by hand without being able to see it. I'd have to come back and do it tomorrow. I felt along the bottom of the reader and switched it off, then got to my feet.

With no light of any kind inside the building, I thought I might be able to see more of what was happening beyond the windows. I peered out, but the center grounds lay shrouded in shadows. Slowly, I picked my way out of the glass enclosure. I'd left the key in the lock, not a good idea I realized now, but to my relief I grabbed hold of it without knocking it loose and locked the door.

I stretched out a hand in front of me as I felt my way into the main room. When I reached Diane's desk, I groped along it until I found the drawer and dropped the key to the microfilm room back in its place.

As I crept into the entrance hall, a flash of lightning revealed that—just as I'd suspected—the front door had blown open and was swinging back and forth, buffeted by the wind. I was reaching for the handle when a dark shape loomed on the steps outside, filling the doorway.

My breath caught in my throat. The shape morphed into a figure with a dark hood pulled up over its head, obscuring the face. I couldn't make out any features, nothing I could recognize. Only an indistinct, dark form, an ominous presence, like the figure on the bluff I'd seen peering down at my house the night after Millicent's party.

No one should be coming to the center at this hour. I backed up and fumbled along the counter, feeling for something I could use as a weapon. My fingers scraped the edge of a ceramic pot Diane had brought in, a decorative planter shaped like a frog which held dried flowers and greenery. I grabbed it and dumped the contents, heard stones and branches tumble out and scatter along the floor. I stuck my right fist deep into the frog, ready to hit and run, hoping I could reach my car and lock the doors while the intruder was too stunned to chase me.

Every muscle in my body tensed as adrenalin powered me for fight or flight. I reared back, lifted the planter high and, at the last minute, grabbed it with both hands, ready to swing it sideways like a misshapen baseball bat toward the hooded shape only a few feet away.

Before I could make my move, the overhead lights flashed on. I jumped. My heart pounded. I squinted against the sudden brightness. The blower on the furnace roared to life. The figure in the doorway, blinking in the glare of the entrance lights, gaped at me, dumbfounded. I stared back, too astonished to lower the planter.

Don Morrison, the hood of his parka flipped up around his head, his face sunburned after his weeks in Hawaii, reached across the space between us and lifted the frog pot out of my hands.

THIRTEEN

THE FIRST THING the next morning I called Diane Anderson and asked her to meet me for a quick supper that night at Mario's Pizzeria. Since we'd been there together the evening before, she realized at once there was something I wanted to talk to her about. Like the good friend she was, she asked no questions and agreed immediately. As soon as we'd settled ourselves in a back booth and ordered wine and Caesar salads, I took her step-by-step through my experience at the center.

Diane listened without comment, but I could sense her mounting astonishment as I related the gossipy accounts I'd found in the old *Emerald Pointers* which detailed Millicent and Carl Durocher's activities. When I described the onslaught of the storm and the loss of power, she reacted with surprise, concern and assurances that she too would have hated being alone in the center at night with no lights.

But when I got to the unexpected arrival of Don Morrison—more accurately the appearance of the hooded dark specter which turned out to be Don Morrison—and my failed attempt to smash him over the head with her ceramic planter, Diane's face twisted into a series of grimaces.

"Wait. You've got to give me a minute here," she gasped finally as she shoved her plate away and surrendered herself to the guffaws of laughter she'd been fighting to suppress.

"It wasn't all that funny, you know," I snapped. I sounded ugly as a bear, but I couldn't help myself.

"Only you, Loren. Didn't you tell me you saw a hooded figure outside Millicent Halstead's place the night of her party? Now you've seen another one? And after you promised the sheriff's department to keep your nose clean. This couldn't happen to anyone but you."

As she succumbed to another laughing fit, she pulled clumps of paper napkins out of the chrome holder and wadded them against her mouth in a desperate effort to stifle the sounds pouring out of her.

While I continued glowering at her across the table, Diane gulped several times, straightened up in her seat and motioned for me to continue. "I'm sorry. Go on."

Before I could speak, she was hit by another spasm of giggles.

I waited.

"The ceramic frog," she muttered when she could finally get words out. "What if you'd hit him with it? Can you imagine the headlines? You'd never have lived it down."

"I know. I know. And somehow that only makes me madder."

"Wait. Let me try to take this more seriously. Go back to the part when the lights came on. At an opportune moment, I'd say, or you could have killed him. What did you say to him?"

"I asked him what the hell he was doing there. Understand my heart was thumping so I could hardly get any words out, much less choose the most appropriate."

Diane clenched her jaw in an effort to keep her face rigid, but I could see a nerve twitch in her cheek. "And he said…"

"Some dumb thing about a long lost warrior hoping for a better greeting on his return. And then he asked me what the hell I was doing there myself."

"Went right on the offensive, did he? How did you explain that?"

"I didn't. I said I'd asked him first." Even I had to admit how childish that remark sounded, but Diane was smart enough not to say so, at least not right then.

"And then?"

"He said—and he spoke very slowly and patiently as if I were deranged—he'd just come home from Hawaii and left messages on my machine about going out for dinner. He'd finally telephoned you, and you told him where I'd gone."

"It was all right for me to tell him, wasn't it? Silly

me. I actually thought you'd be glad he was home." She caught the side of her lower lip between her teeth and gave it a pinch.

"I know. I know. I should have been. The whole thing was so crazy. He wanted to go some place to eat, except by then it was almost eleven o'clock. I don't think this time of year any restaurant around here would still be serving."

"Except this one, of course." Diane waved her hand to encompass Mario's booths and tables.

"I'd just left here, remember? Anyway I was tired and ready to call it a night. So I asked for a rain check and went home."

"Without inviting him along?"

"Don't even think about lecturing me on that subject. I can't tell you why I didn't suggest making him a sandwich at my house, or even if I was sorry afterward I didn't."

"You're going to need Dr. Phil for this one, Loren. We moved out of my realm of expertise a long time ago. I say you call him, invite him for one of your home cooked dinners from Kate's and get things back on track."

"Not that easy. He's gone to Albany for a post-conference recap. He'll be there for a couple of days. But don't worry. I'll figure things out sooner or later." I signaled our waitress for the check.

Diane stood up and pulled on her jacket. "You might want to keep in mind what Shakespeare said about that guy who threw the pearl away richer than all his tribe."

"You're suggesting he meant that for women too? I love hanging around with an English teacher. You offer advice in such a classy way I can hardly ignore it."

"Then don't." Diane turned on her heel and marched out of the restaurant ahead of me.

FOURTEEN

"LOREN, I ASSUME you received the check from my accountant."

When Millicent Halstead telephoned my office the next morning, she spoke in her usual assured manner, but something in her tone told me she already knew what I was going to say.

"Did he tell you he sent it?" I asked.

"That's why I'm calling. He's away this week, but he promised he'd mail it out to you before he left."

"Apparently he didn't."

"I so hoped I could count on him. I've been asked to speak to a group at the Emerald Point Inn this evening. Members of a New York State department in Albany are holding a three-day conference there, and the speaker scheduled for tonight has cancelled on them. I'm really embarrassed about the check from last time, but could I possibly talk you into selling books for me again tonight?"

I hesitated long enough for Millicent to realize I wasn't jumping at the chance.

"You're probably wondering if I'm all talk about

turning over the profits from the sales, but I do hope you'll trust me for a few more days. I can get the books to the Inn myself, so if you could just meet me there around seven."

My mind raced through possible reasons to refuse. I'd thought about scheduling a committee meeting for tonight. Why hadn't I done it?"

"This is a real opportunity for me," Millicent went on. "These are women from all over New York State and if they go home with my book…well, I can't buy advertising like that."

I caved.

As I DROVE TO the Emerald Point Inn that night, I was experiencing more than my fair share of misgivings, and not simply because of my doubts about Millicent. I didn't go to the Inn very often these days. To be honest, I never went if I could get out of it, but my reasons were personal and had nothing to do with the Inn's ability to host a great conference. The large meeting rooms made an ideal location for corporate training sessions, and the hotel's modern amenities combined with its 19th century charm usually assured owner John Roberts of a satisfied clientele.

When I arrived, I found Millicent totally in command. She'd located the room where she was to speak and commandeered a small table near the door for sales. Someone had carried in several boxes of her books for her, and she'd already arranged a dozen copies on the table. A colorful new poster featured accolades even more glowing than those we'd displayed at the last sale.

Millicent thanked me again for coming and pointed to the money box tucked discreetly on a chair behind the sales table. Then she rushed off to the podium at the front of the room.

As the conference attendees filed in, I realized she'd be facing a totally different audience tonight than the one at the Lake George Club. These women were well-paid, no-nonsense professionals, already a little disgruntled by the cancellation of the scheduled speaker. The remarks I overheard didn't bode well for Millicent's reception.

"Who did you say this person is?" someone asked a companion as they walked by me.

"Some local. I don't know why they bothered. They might better have let us socialize or do some of that reading they've given us."

As soon as the meeting room was three-quarters full, Millicent detached the microphone from the podium and took command. "I'm Millicent Halstead. I know you're disappointed about not hearing Marianne Hathaway tonight. I'm afraid only our initials are the same. My topic will be totally different from the subject she was going to speak on. So go ahead and groan if you want to. Let's get that out of the way right now."

She spoke in such a pleasant, straightforward way

several of the women chuckled. Others offered a few good-natured groans which led to more laughter.

"And to rub salt in the wound," Millicent continued, "I know Marianne; I've heard her speak a number of times and she's a spellbinder. But I hope I have something to offer, something different, but still worthwhile. My understanding is that most of you are required to travel for your work. You've done it in the past; you'll be doing more of it in the future; and you might like to swap ideas on how to make your trips as pain-free as possible, especially now that travel has become so much more difficult since 9/11.

"So if you can just switch gears, I'll kick off with a few anecdotes from my book about my own experiences. Then I'll be asking for contributions from anyone who wants to chime in."

To my surprise, the women in the audience perked up, sat up straighter and appeared to listen. True to her word, Millicent kept her remarks brief and focused on women traveling on business.

When she called for comments from the floor, she lucked out. One of the women stood and told a humorous story about getting on a plane bound for Portland, Oregon, when she was going to Portland, Maine. "The two planes were leaving at almost the same time from adjacent gates. Can you imagine?"

Millicent laughed appreciatively. "I suspect we've all had near misses, and even without that kind of assistance from the airlines. It's easy to misread departure times, gate numbers, other information key to the success of the trip. The most important thing is to take control ourselves, not leave it to others."

This led to an exchange of comments from women in the audience on dealing with the increased restrictions. Millicent encouraged their participation and at the same time kept anyone from monopolizing the discussion. When she concluded the program after an hour, she received a respectable round of applause and a dozen or more women hurried back to purchase a book and take it to be signed.

Well done, I thought. A tough audience, and she had them on her side in no time.

After the last sale, I'd arranged the bills in the strong box and was counting the small pile of coins when a low voice behind me murmured in my ear. "Loren Graham, what the hell are you up to now?"

I froze. I didn't have to look up to know who was hovering over my left shoulder, standing too close, the way he liked to do, invading my space, sending strange, but familiar, sensations along my nerves and—I didn't have a doubt in the world—knowing only too well he was doing it.

I swung around and faced Jack Roberts. I swallowed hard and attempted a casual hello.

"Hello, yourself. I want to know who this dame is and what you're doing selling books for her," he said.

Even now in his forties, Jack hadn't lost the movie star looks, damn him. More than two years since I'd seen him, and he still had the physique of a guy who worked out every chance he got. His hair, always one of his best features, was the same thick, dark brown I remembered from when I'd first known him years ago. His face, craggy and unlined, still showed traces of his usual summer tan.

I kept things light. "One of the many good deeds I perform for the citizens of Emerald Point. Always the dedicated public servant."

"Good deeds come in some really strange packages, it looks like."

I redirected the conversation. "More to the point, what the hell are you doing here?"

"Why don't I buy you a drink in the bar and tell you all about it?"

Before I could answer, Millicent came barreling down on us. A good-looking, sexy guy was a magnet to her, I'd noticed at her last talk, and Jack Roberts scored high points in both categories.

I made the introductions.

"I've been dealing with a Mr. John Roberts. Would you be a member of the family who owns this hotel?" She glanced up at Jack with a coquettish smile.

"You're very perceptive. That would be my father," he said, oozing charm.

Millicent blushed at the compliment, then bubbled on

about her book and her pleasure at the audience's response.

Jack made no move to interrupt, even bent his head closer to her, as if anxious not to miss a word.

As I shifted from one foot to another, an unexpected movement in the hallway outside the conference room attracted my attention. Out of the corner of my eye I saw Arthur Blake creeping slowly along, escorting his mother down the hall.

Why? I wondered. *Why would they be here tonight?* For years now, Mrs. Blake had seldom left her house. Yet this was the second time in the last two weeks I'd seen her-first at Millicent's party and now here.

As the Blakes disappeared through a rear door, Jack and Millicent, boon companions by this time, drifted toward the bar.

"Do come along, Loren," Millicent called back to me over her shoulder, "especially now that we have this charming escort."

Jack turned around to give me a quick wink.

At that moment I could have announced I needed to leave, pleaded some urgent matter waiting for me at home, but I hesitated and, as we entered the bar, I realized I'd let the moment for gracious leave-taking pass.

Jack pulled out chairs for us both at a small table, assured himself we were comfortable, then asked what we wanted to drink. He crossed the room and gave the order to the attractive young woman tending bar, who dimpled and set up a tray with two wine glasses and a dish of nuts.

Jack brought the tray over, positioned cocktail napkins and the nuts on the table and placed glasses of white wine in front of us both.

"I'm sorry I can't join you, ladies. Perhaps another time," he said.

"Oh no. You're leaving? You can't stay even a few minutes?" Millicent sounded as if she might burst into tears.

"I enjoyed meeting you, Millicent. And Loren, always good to see you." Jack spun out a few more meaningless phrases and sauntered off toward the door we'd come through, nodding and smiling at other women in the bar as he left.

A perfectly executed departure. A microcosm of every experience I'd ever had with Jack Roberts. The charming overture, the promise of a something more and then, as soon as he sensed he'd reeled me in with that phony charisma, the cold dash of reality.

As I half-listened to Millicent ramble on about her talk, I couldn't decide which made me angrier—Jack's manipulation or the fact that I'd come close to being taken in one more time.

In a few minutes, Millicent interrupted her recap to ask, "We should have another, don't you think?"

Before I could object, she signaled to the bartender.

I shook my head at the girl, but that didn't stop her from sending a bus boy over with another glass for Millicent.

"Compliments of Mr. Roberts," he muttered as he set the drink down.

By this time, most of the women from the conference had drifted off to their rooms. Six or eight remained at the tables in the window, apparently mesmerized by the view of the lake and the lights twinkling along the shore below us. The bus boy moved quietly among the tables, picking up empty glasses.

Maybe if Jack hadn't pulled his old bait and switch, if Millicent hadn't delayed our departure by ordering another drink, if I'd just been able to go home and call it a night, I would have kept my mouth shut.

But I didn't. Even before Millicent had wound down, I opened the can of worms—the subject I knew would be a hot topic. "I came across some articles about you and Carl Durocher."

She beamed. "You did? Where? I've been hoping to get some publicity in the papers around here."

"Nothing recent, I'm afraid. These were in a little newspaper called *Emerald Pointers*."

She didn't manage to hide her surprise, although I sensed she was trying. "You mean that piece of garbage is still being published?"

"Not as far as I know. These were issues from years back."

"I hope you realize you can't believe a word in them.

That paper was nothing but a scandal sheet. They were finally sued out of business, I heard." Her hand shook as she picked up her wine glass.

I waited, didn't say more.

"What type of article did you happen on? Accounts of wild parties, some wife-swapping thrown in maybe?"

"Something like that."

"I hate thinking those stories are still out there. That editor hated Carl, did everything in his power to besmirch his reputation."

"Even when the stories didn't have any basis in fact?"

She gave me a sharp look, took another swallow of wine. "Loren, I think you know they did. Carl had quite the reputation in those years. Some of his biographers have hinted at it. More than hinted in some cases."

I wasn't sure what to say. I'd read articles in the *Times* and other papers about Carl Durocher's life and work. Some of the less scholarly accounts had included uncomplimentary details about his personal life, but this was not the time for a heart-to-heart on that subject, if I wanted to get out of here.

I tried to redirect the conversation. "This must have been very painful for you," I said.

"Actually, that was part of the reason we didn't stay at the lake very long. I loved living here for a while, but things happened. After almost thirty years, I thought it was safe to come back."

She didn't know Emerald Point very well if she'd thought that. I bit down on my tongue, but it refused to be silenced. "And now you don't think so?"

"I thought if I came back here, the past would be forgotten. But people won't let it go. I saw someone again tonight, someone who I just know is going to make trouble for me."

I had to ask. "Do you mean Victoria Blake?"

"Victoria?" she scoffed. "Plain Vicky Blake she was when I knew her. I heard years ago she'd died. When I asked the real estate agent about her, he told me she was a recluse, never went out of the house. Now she's turned up twice. Ruining my party wasn't enough for her. She had to come here to spoil my talk."

How had she managed that? I wondered. "I did notice her in the hall tonight, but she wasn't in the room when you gave your talk."

"No. Of course not. That's not Vicky's style. She'd rather hover around like a ghost."

"When I saw her at your party, I assumed you'd been friends in the past."

"Friends? Vicky Blake doesn't have friends." She swung around in her chair and called to the bartender. "We need more drinks here."

Before the young woman could reach for the wine, I countermanded the order. "Never mind. We have to call it a night."

"Oh, Loren, it's not that late," Millicent protested.

I didn't listen. I pulled out money for a tip and stood next to the table until she got to her feet. "It's time to go. You can ride home with me."

"I'll do no such thing. I can drive. I'm perfectly all right."

She steadied herself against the edge of the table, then grabbed my arm and leaned against me. Neither of us said anything more as we picked our way out of the bar and down the hall toward the door.

Millicent Halstead's past had come back to haunt her.

But then, so had mine.

FIFTEEN

IN THE PARKING LOT Millicent kept insisting she was perfectly capable of driving, even while I guided her away from her own car and toward mine.

I opened the door of my Saab and eased her into the passenger seat. "I'm sure you don't want a DWI, Millicent. Imagine how that would look in the papers. You can pick up your car tomorrow."

To my surprise, she stopped protesting and leaned back. "I suppose you're right. At least I'm not taking you out of your way."

She didn't speak again on the ride home, but when we reached Cove Road, she straightened up in the seat and turned to me. Her voice was clearer. "Loren, I can't tell you how sorry I am about this. Seeing Vicky Blake upset me. Maybe I shouldn't have come back to Emerald Point. It's been so long since I lived here, I assumed people would have forgotten all about me."

I started to ask how she could assume such a thing, but bit back the words. I thought like a native now. I sometimes lost track of the fact others might not.

Millicent went on musing, almost to herself. "When

we lived here, Vicky was obsessed with Carl. She wouldn't stay away from him."

I did some fast mental arithmetic. "Mrs. Blake? Wouldn't she have been a lot older than you and Carl?"

"A lot older than me, but almost the same age as Carl, actually. He was in his forties then. I was eighteen. We met when I was a student in one of his classes. I dropped out of college to move up here with him."

I thought of Josie Donohue. Could Millicent have been as naïve and scatter-brained as Josie and some of her friends? Had she been easy prey for an unscrupulous professor? I felt a rush of sympathy for her.

"You and Carl were married when you moved here?"

"We married when he found out I was pregnant. That was my hold over him. I was going to give Carl the one thing in this world he wanted more than anything else, even more than recognition as a poet—his own child. He'd been married twice, had numerous affairs. Doctors had told him time and again he'd never have children. Then suddenly, I was pregnant."

"That must have been a surprise to both of you," I said, choosing my words carefully.

"At first, I was afraid to tell him, afraid he'd think I'd cheated on him, even though I was seldom out of his sight. But he accepted the pregnancy, not just accepted it, but was overjoyed. He insisted we marry immediately before we moved to the lake for his sabbatical."

We pulled up in front of Millicent's house. I

stopped the car and turned to face her. "I didn't realize you had a child."

She set her mouth in a straight line and shoved open the car door. "I didn't. I was five months along when I miscarried. And that changed everything."

"Wait. Let me walk to the door with you." Suddenly she seemed very fragile. I realized talking about Carl and her pregnancy had upset her

"No. I'm all right. I've caused you enough trouble for one night." She mouthed a thank you as she slid out of the car.

I watched as she picked her way up the walk. When I saw her front door close behind her, I breathed a sigh of relief and took off down the hill.

Once home, I made a determined effort to put Millicent and what she'd told me out of my mind, but it took a *Law & Order* rerun, an old Bette Davis movie and two cups of cocoa to make me fall asleep.

THE NEXT MORNING I woke an hour earlier than usual with bits and pieces of my conversation with Millicent still whirling around in my head.

Summer was making a comeback, however brief it might be, and the weather was perfect for a run. The dirt road along the shore was deserted. Once I passed the cellar of the burned-out house, I focused my attention on a Village Board meeting we'd scheduled for that night and shoved the skeleton, Millicent Halstead and

Victoria Blake firmly out of my mind. I even refused to let my recurring thoughts about Jack Roberts spoil the serenity of a glorious fall morning in my favorite part of the world.

The town of Emerald Point hugged a sheltered cove, almost equidistant from the northern reaches of the lake at Ticonderoga and Lake George Village at the southern end. Although many of the stores and businesses in our downtown stayed open through the winter, the day-to-day pace had already slowed with the departure of the summer people.

In early fall even the year-round residents in the elegant lakeside mansions on the northern edge of town cut back their social activities, at least for a time. The groundskeepers stayed busy, trimming trees and bushes and preparing the wide lawns for winter while the local women who worked as cleaners and housekeepers washed windows and moved porch furniture into storage.

With many of the camps along here closed for the winter, this part of the shore was quiet. I drifted into a relaxed state, concentrating only on the pound of my Adidas on the hard-packed dirt.

As I passed the Blake cottage on my return, Arthur yanked open his front door and swooped toward me down his front sidewalk. Was it my imagination, I wondered, or was Arthur beginning to mimic the movements of his favorite subjects?

"Loren," he called. "Wait up a minute. I want to ask you something."

I needed a few seconds to catch my breath. "What is it, Arthur?"

"Our new neighbor, Millicent Halstead. Someone said you were working for her. Is that what you were doing at the Inn last night?" His harsh tone of voice made his feelings on the subject very clear.

I gave him a quick summary of my arrangement with Millicent. "I'm helping her with her book sales, Arthur. In return, she's making a donation toward our rebuilding efforts."

The crevasses on his face deepened as he frowned. "I don't care how big a donation she makes, Loren. You don't want to have anything to do with that woman. She's bad news."

"Really? In what way?" I hedged, not ready to acknowledge my own concerns about Millicent, but curious about what Arthur would say.

"You'll find out. She can't be trusted. If you'd lived around here longer, you'd know."

That ruined it. A remark like that always raised my hackles. How long did I have to live here before people thought I belonged?

"Not good enough, Arthur. You'll have to give me specific reasons if you want to convince me."

"You'll find out. Don't say I didn't warn you." He turned on his heel and darted back up the walk without looking back.

Relaxed state totally shattered.

Once home I indulged myself with a long, hot shower, but it did nothing to improve my mood. Even though I harbored my own doubts about Millicent, I hated being warned away from anyone or anything, especially in vague terms I didn't understand. And yet, Arthur's comments had given me even more to think about.

At the office, I guzzled down two cups of super-strong Vermont blend coffee and dug out a form I'd put off filing with the State. I forced myself to concentrate and whipped through the first three pages in record time. As I reached the summation, I heard a tapping on the outer door.

Millicent Halstead, looking even more sleep-deprived than I felt, shifted awkwardly on the doorstep. Before I could react, she said, "Loren, I promise not to keep you. I've come to apologize for last night and to thank you for getting me home safely. When I think what might have happened if I'd tried to drive myself…well…you'll never know how grateful I am. And I have your check for you finally."

I hoped this wasn't an overture to a heart-to-heart talk, but I couldn't leave her standing on the doorstep. "Come in, Millicent. Sit down. Did you get your car already?"

She followed me into my office, but waved away my offer of a chair. She remained standing as she reached into her pocketbook and handed me an envelope.

"Will drove me to the Inn first thing this morning to pick up my car and the unsold books. Then I went directly to the bank and arranged for your commission from the book sales."

I opened the envelope and stared at the amount written on the check. "You don't owe me this much, Millicent. Did your accountant figure this for you?"

"He's still out of town, Loren, but I didn't want you to wait any longer. You've done everything I asked. If this is more than we agreed on, you earned it. I know you'll use it in a good cause." She swung around fast and headed toward the door.

"Millicent…" I started to protest. Before I could say more, she'd yanked open the front door and rushed out.

The $1000 on the check exceeded anything I'd expected from the book sales, anything I'd thought Millicent might donate to our recovery efforts. In fact, it could very well be more than the amount she'd made herself.

Why was she doing this? Was it because she was embarrassed about her over-indulgence last night or did she have some other reason?

I knew I should be grateful for her generosity. I knew the town could put the money to good use. Then why couldn't I shake the feeling I'd just been bought and paid for?

SIXTEEN

THE FIRST TIME I SAW Kate Donohue prepare for a major catering effort, I'd resolved to apply the techniques she used to my own disorganized approach to life. First, Kate made a detailed list of everything which had to be done, ranked the jobs in order of importance and time required, and prepared a schedule for when each task should be started and completed. During the days preceding the event, she dealt with each job in the proper order and checked it off as she finished it.

After I'd tried this technique in my work life with good results, I determined to incorporate it into my personal life as well. Although I failed on the follow-through more often than not, the week after Millicent's appearance at the Inn, I set about making a plan which I thought would help me whip my life into better shape. I began with a jumbled, half-formed list which cried out for organization.

1. Find out more about the skeleton.

2. Find out if anyone besides me had seen the figure on the bluff the night of Millicent's party.

3. Discover what Jim meant when he suggested I ask Josie Donohue about the cellar of the burned-out house.

4. Decide what to do about Millicent, including whether or not to keep her donation, continue to help at future talks or question her about her stay at the lake years ago. (This last only to satisfy my own curiosity.)

5. Quit creating stumbling blocks with Don and get our relationship back on track.

I didn't need a psychiatrist to tell me I'd relegated the most important matter to last place. But one thing I'd learned over the years was that when you tackle a list, it may not be a good idea to start with the most difficult task. So I opted for a chat with Josie Donohue about the cellar.

"Good. You're home," I said the next afternoon when she answered my knock at her door an hour after school let out.

She glared at me. "Only because I'm grounded. When my mother comes back, would you speak to her about her out-of-date ideas, Lor? I'm sure if you had a kid, you wouldn't be so unreasonable."

The remark smacked of a compliment, but I knew better than to fall for it. Instead I tried for a sympathetic look and asked, "Did you do something you shouldn't have?"

"Curfews suck," she growled. "Will you tell me how a parent can refuse to let you take the car, then get bent out of shape when you have to ride with someone else and that makes you late getting home?"

"Beats me. Nobody else to ask for a ride, I take it."

Josie snorted. "I was right near you. I could of woke you up, Lor, but I didn't think you'd go much for that."

The conversation had drifted right where I wanted it to go. "Oh, were you in my neighborhood?" I asked, all innocence and guile.

Josie was too smart to admit to that. She cast a sidelong look in my direction and didn't answer.

"Like maybe you and your friends were in a cellar near me, fixing it up to use as a hangout. Something like that?"

"So what if, Lor? Kids do stuff like that all the time, don't they? Wouldn't be anything so wrong with it, would there?" The look she gave me indicated she was serious, maybe even a little scared.

"I don't know all the details, but if you guys would lie low for a couple of weeks, especially while there's an investigation going on…"

"You think?"

"Or maybe you could go to the sheriff's department and tell them what you know. Might be good psychology to talk to them before they come looking for you."

"Even if we don't know anything?"

"Just in case somebody thinks you might," I said.

"You could have a point," she conceded. "I'll give it some thought."

Seed planted.

SEVENTEEN

ONE OF THE MAJOR IRONIES in my life was that while I sometimes thought I knew how Josie could solve her problems, I often turned to her mother for help in resolving my own.

"I've kind of messed up with Don and I'm not sure how to get back on track," I admitted to Kate that afternoon when I stopped by the coffee shop.

"Perhaps you should apply my patented way to a man's heart strategy," Kate said. "It involves food and it's usually very successful. Although now that I think about it, the approach has worked better with my customers than for me personally."

"Kate, I'm sure it would work equally well for you if you found someone you wanted to apply it to. So think of Don as a guinea pig."

"Didn't you say he liked that new boeuf bourguignon I've been making? I've got a portion for two in the freezer. You can have it bubbling in your hot pot in no time. Mushrooms and vegetables are already in it. I've got those rolls he likes too. All you'll have to do is add a salad, and you're in business. You could have a couple of slices of chocolate cheese cake in reserve, but I bet you won't get to dessert before he has other things on his mind."

"I wish I had your confidence. I'm not even sure he'll come if I call and invite him to dinner."

"Then go to his house. Take my big picnic basket. Much more romantic than dragging in with a cooler."

Kate pulled packets out of the freezer and arranged them on the counter in front of her. Then she reached up to a high shelf for an old-fashioned wicker picnic basket lined with blue and white checked gingham.

"Now I'm packing everything in here as is," she explained. "But you'll want to heat the stew in your big hot pot when you get home. Make sure it's bubbling when you put the pot in the basket. Then snuggle the rolls up next to it so they'll thaw and warm. Keep the cheesecake in your refrigerator and add it just as you leave."

"I've got wine I can bring and I'll make a salad while your main course is heating. You're a lifesaver, Kate. Thank you." I pulled bills out of my wallet and slid them under a sugar bowl on the counter. Paying Kate always required a little trickery.

I glanced at my watch as I drove home. Not five o'clock yet. Time to heat and, repack the food and get to Don's before he started his own dinner. If, of course, he planned to eat at home, and alone. Imagine my embarrassment if I marched in with my gourmet meal and found him entertaining another woman. Well this wasn't the time to worry about something like that.

As I pulled into my yard, I noticed an unfamiliar car parked across the street. Before I'd opened my trunk, Jack Roberts swung out of the car, and sauntered across the yard toward me.

Damn. I had to hand it to him. The man not only didn't age, he still knew how to dress. A classy looking beige windbreaker over brown slacks and sport shirt. I wouldn't be surprised if he had a personal shopper.

He speeded up when he saw me lifting the basket out of the trunk. "Hang on, Loren. Let me help you with that."

The basket wasn't heavy, but there seemed no reason to refuse. I handed it over.

He followed me up the path to the back door and into the kitchen.

As soon as he'd set the basket on the table, he swung around to face me. "Loren, I've come to apologize for ducking out on you the other night at the Inn. I wanted to talk with you, but I couldn't handle a conversation with that woman hanging on every word. What's her name? Millicent? I still don't understand what you were doing with her."

We stood on opposite sides of the kitchen table and stared across it at one another. I didn't answer. I didn't owe him any explanation.

Jack broke the impasse. He slid into a chair at the table. "Mind if I sit?"

I didn't point out he'd already done that. I turned and reached down into a low cupboard to pull out my crock pot. "Let me start this heating, and then we can talk. You sound like a man with something on his mind."

To my surprise, Jack stumbled over his reply—a real first. "Maybe I should have called you or made an appointment to come to your office. I don't seem to be thinking very clearly these days."

"Is something wrong?" I emptied Kate's packets into the crock pot and plugged it in.

He didn't answer for a minute, but waited until I'd sat down across from him. Then he said, "Nothing more than usual, I suppose. Missed opportunities. Trying to figure out how to go back and undo mistakes."

Something was definitely wrong. This wasn't a typical Jack Roberts pronouncement, at least not to me. "If you can figure out how to do that and tell the rest of us, your fortune will be made. Is your father becoming a problem again?"

"You mean with wild schemes like he was hatching a couple years ago? No, but he's slowing down. He could use help, but he doesn't want it. Doesn't want help, doesn't want advice, doesn't want anything from anybody."

This had been a familiar theme with Jack and his father as long as I could remember. "From anybody, or just from you?"

"Loren, you still have that knack for zeroing in on what's wrong. What did you use to call it—defining the problem?"

"I get a lot of practice doing that nowadays."

"And we both know defining a problem is only the first step. I suppose things can't be easy for you either. I asked somebody who was on your council this term. You've got a couple of tough characters to deal with. Darren Jones—he can grind on a subject until he gets everyone's head spinning."

"You know Darren, I take it?" I left it at that. In politics, even a casual remark to an old friend could lead to trouble if passed on to the wrong person at the wrong time. I'd learned that the hard way.

I couldn't tell where the conversation was heading, but maybe a beer would speed it along. I walked over to the refrigerator and took two cans out of the lower drawer. When I held them up for Jack's approval, he nodded with enthusiasm.

"That woman you were with the other night. Did you know she's an old acquaintance of my father's?" he asked.

I opened the beers and handed him one. "I know she lived here years ago."

"More than an acquaintance in fact. Part of the reason behind my parents' divorce as I understand it." He downed half his beer fast and waited for my reaction.

I was stunned. I was never good at hiding my shock at pronouncements like that, so I didn't try. "Really? Your father told you that?'

"No, of course not. And my mother doesn't talk

about what happened either. But my uncle's told some pretty wild stories. Can't swear they're all true…"

Did that mean Jack had heard the old gossip? "I've seen some newspapers from years ago called *Emerald Pointers*. Not sure how much of what appeared in their gossip columns was true either, but Millicent and Carl Durocher, the man she was married to then, apparently ran with a wild crowd. Do you think your father was part of that?"

"There's some reason my father was a no-show the other night when that woman spoke at the Inn. Not like him to hide out in his room when there's a visitor from the old days downstairs."

"Do you think that's what he was doing, hiding out to avoid Millicent?"

"It sure looked that way." He turned and glanced back toward the counter. "What in heaven's name are you cooking? I didn't have any lunch today and that smell's got my insides churning."

"That's not a smell. That's an aroma. Maybe it's time you learned the difference."

I scooped some of Kate's boeuf bourguignon onto a plate and popped it into the microwave. In a couple of minutes, it was steaming hot. I slid a place mat and silverware onto the table and set the plate in front of Jack.

He couldn't lap it up fast enough. "My God, do you eat like this all the time? I either order something off the menu at the Inn—where the entrees have gotten very old hat, by the way—or I make myself a grilled cheese sandwich. That's the only cooking I've mastered."

Once again, I saw no need to explain details of my life to Jack Roberts. I warmed a packet of rolls, heated more of the beef in the microwave and served him a giant-sized portion. Then, because the aroma was getting to me too, I pulled out another place mat and plate and dished up a helping of Kate's savory concoction for myself.

Before I sat down again, I opened one of the bottles of Merlot I'd planned to bring to Don's and poured us each a glass. A barely audible voice in my head pointed out that the first stage of betrayal was always the easiest.

By eight o'clock, we'd wolfed down as much of Kate's boeuf bourguignon as two people could possibly manage, opened the other bottle of wine and split one of the slices of chocolate cheesecake. After I'd put what was left of the food into the refrigerator, we decided it was warm enough outside to move to the screened porch.

"This was always one of the prettiest spots on the lake," Jack said as he settled into my grandmother's hammock. He'd been full of compliments all evening— the food, the wine, how much he was enjoying reliving our shared memories of the old days at the lake.

I did some reminiscing of my own. "I loved spending summers here with my grandparents. Then when my grandfather died and left the house to me, I kept thinking I should sell it and go back to New York. Remember? And I just couldn't bring myself to do it. This place casts a spell."

"And it's been a good choice for you." Jack disentangled himself from the hammock and walked over to the rocker where I was sitting. He lifted the glass out of my hand and set it on the railing. Then he seized my wrists and pulled me gently to my feet.

He was standing too close again. I caught the faint hint of his aftershave, the smell of the Merlot on his breath. The muscles in my throat contracted. How many times had I imagined standing with him this way one more time, feeling his body close to mine? I thought about moving away from him, but I didn't do it.

He let go of my wrists and slid his arms slowly around my waist. The quick tug that pulled me against him ignited a familiar burn deep inside me. He was taller than Don. My head fit comfortably in the hollow below his shoulder. His body felt hard and muscular, no different than it had felt years ago. The smooth cotton fabric of his shirt caressed my cheek. I could have stood like this forever.

But forever wasn't Jack's way. He took my chin in his hand and turned my face up to his. The porch was dark now. Only the light from the kitchen illuminated the doorway and laid an amber shaft across the wide wooden planks of the porch floor. He gave me a long, assessing look and bent to kiss me.

The kiss lingered, built in intensity, brought a rush of memories, promised something more. But it demanded nothing. At least for the moment, he was offering me the chance to decide where it would lead. That gentleness, so unlike the Jack I'd known in the past, compelled me more than insistence would have.

The attraction which had smoldered between us for so long flashed brighter, incandescent as the sudden flash of lightning, pulsing across the northern sky. The force of my reaction startled me. I leaned into him, savoring the moment, wanting these feelings to last.

He moved back toward the hammock and pulled me down next to him. He swept my hair back, then cradled my face in his hands. His fingers burned. He tilted my face up and kissed me again, more urgently this time.

"Loren, I didn't mean to hurt you. I'm sorry. I can't tell you how many times I've regretted it."

The lie, offered so easily, broke the spell. I sat up. The hammock creaked as I slid away from him. "Jack, that happened a long time ago. We were different people then."

"Loren, wait…I want to say something."

"I'm getting my drink."

I slipped off the hammock and stood up. I retrieved my glass from the low table where he'd set it. The drink was nothing but melted ice now, but I drained the glass. I didn't go back to the hammock.

I couldn't know exactly what Jack wanted to say, but one thing I was sure of—I no longer wanted to hear it.

Before I could find a way to stop him, I heard a sharp snap in the side yard as if someone had stepped on a dry stick. For a long moment there was silence, then the soft rustle of footsteps. A shadow flickered against the bushes. I moved quickly toward the edge of the porch. It wasn't my imagination—there was someone out there. The figure pressed further back into the darkness, groping for a way through the overgrown shrubs. Someone had been out there in the shadows of the yard, watching me again.

EIGHTEEN

"WHO IS IT? WHO'S THERE?" I made my voice sound harsh, authoritative. At least I tried to.

Jack crossed the porch and stood next to me. "What's going on?"

"Somebody's standing out there in the bushes. I guess I'd better call the sheriff's department." I spoke loudly enough to be heard.

Arthur Blake stepped forward, shoving branches aside. "No, don't do that, Loren, at least not yet."

"Arthur, what in the world? Watching bats is fine, but not if you scare your neighbors to death while you're doing it."

"I didn't mean to startle you. I knocked at your kitchen door, but you didn't answer. I heard you on the porch. I need you to help me. Meet me in your backyard." Without waiting for my response, he slipped back through the bushes.

"I'll have to see what he wants," I told Jack.

"Loren, I probably shouldn't have come. I...I..."

His last apology had gone so poorly, I understood his reluctance to offer another, but I didn't help him out.

Instead I hurried ahead of him through the house and out the kitchen door into the yard. "What is it, Arthur? Is your mother ill?"

"No. Nothing like that. She's disappeared. I've searched everywhere and she's gone. I don't know where she can be."

Definitely not my night. I followed Arthur across the grass to the road that ran past his house, the same road I'd taken the night Darla led me into the cellar of the old house where the Blakes had once lived.

Arthur stopped suddenly and began swinging his flashlight back and forth along the grass. "She's disappeared. I thought she might be wandering around here where there's more light."

We'd reached his house. The light Arthur was talking about came from his backyard, where the bulbs he turned on at night to attract the bats hung from wires stretched between the trees.

Jack followed along behind me. He kept his voice low so Arthur didn't hear him. "Loren, you don't need me for this, do you? I'll go now unless you want me to hang around."

We both knew the answer to that.

"No. It's all right. I want to give Arthur a hand. His mother's probably somewhere close by, but he's worried about her."

As Jack made good his escape, I took my emotional temperature. I expected to feel at least a twinge of regret, a sadness that something that had once seemed so important was finally over. There was nothing. If I felt any emotion at all, it appeared so briefly I couldn't identify it.

Arthur tramped back and forth through the yards bordering the road. He seemed to be more anxious each time he returned. "Loren, what should I do? I can't imagine where she's gone. And we're going to get a bad storm."

"Take it easy, Arthur. Tell me exactly what happened."

"I was outside earlier. I watched the bats in my yard for a while and then I went in to record some sightings. The ones I saw tonight were mostly the small brown bats. They'll be gone soon—gone into hibernation. I want to take more notes on the vampire bats too before winter. If I could get out to George McCauley's farm again…he's found some of his cattle bleeding. He thinks vampire bats are getting on them at night."

Under other circumstances, I might have asked questions on that subject, but right now, we didn't have time for it. "What about your mother, Arthur? You'd gone back inside the house and…"

"I heard voices, kids' voices. I went back out to tell them to be quiet. I've heard them off and on all summer. Kids coming down the road late, and cars starting up. I don't like it, Loren. They shouldn't be out this late, especially now that school's started."

"Probably not, but keep going. You went out when

you heard the voices. That wasn't a good idea, Arthur. Even if they were kids, you were alone and probably outnumbered."

"I know. I know. But sometimes they wake Mother, and then it takes an hour or more to settle her down. And worse, she's gone out by herself a couple of times to see what's going on. I bet she did that tonight—went out to check. That's why I have Darla staying with us. She's supposed to watch Mother when I go out to do my observations. And I need to do some more counting for my records."

I didn't know what he meant by his records, but I wanted him to focus on the subject at hand. I grabbed his arm. "Arthur, tell me. Do you think Darla is with her right now?"

"I don't know. I'm starting to realize I can't always trust Darla. I think she goes out herself sometimes, after I think she's in bed for the night."

I had a feeling he was right about that. Hadn't Darla done that very thing the night she took me to see the skeleton? But at this point, our first concern was Victoria and where she'd disappeared to.

"What was your mother wearing?" I asked him.

"Nightgown and robe probably, unless she got all dressed again. She'd gone into her room to get ready for bed."

I didn't like that answer. Even during this warm spell, the temperature dropped at night. The air already had a nip to it. If Victoria wasn't wearing a jacket or coat, she'd be chilled through very quickly.

Arthur and I continued down the road, then turned back to search yards and culverts we'd skipped before. We saw no signs of Victoria herself or anything that would indicate she'd been out here. Arthur became more agitated. "Loren, maybe I should call the sheriff's department and report her missing," he said finally.

A vision of Investigator Thompson's face appeared in the trees above me like one of those frightening images from the Apocalypse. I came up with an alternative plan fast.

"Arthur, why don't you check your house one more time? Your mother may have gone in the back door when we couldn't see her. We want to be sure before we call the sheriff's department. If she's not there, maybe we could walk up to Cove Road and knock on a few doors."

Several year-round families lived on Cove Road near Millicent Halstead's place. I realized it was late to intrude on people, but that would be a logical next step.

"But shouldn't I call the sheriff's department first?" Arthur, visibly shaken, pleaded for my okay.

This time I flashed on Deputy Rick Cronin driving all the way from wherever he was assigned tonight to hear a report, not of a skeleton but of a disappearance, and probably a disappearance of someone who'd turned up by the time he got here. That didn't seem like a good idea either.

"I think we should at least check your house first," I said in my best take-command voice.

His lined face relaxed a little. "If you think so."

We started up his front walk. As we reached the porch, Darla Phillips swung open the front door and put a finger to her lips for quiet. "Arthur, your mother insisted on wandering around outside again," she whispered. "I couldn't talk her out of it, so I went with her. She's back now and almost asleep. You probably shouldn't wake her."

Arthur collapsed against the doorjamb as if he might faint with relief. "Loren, thank you, thank you," he whispered.

I started to leave, then turned back. "You'll call it a night too, won't you Arthur? I don't think you should go back out by yourself tonight. You seem so tired."

"You don't have to worry about that. I can't wait to get to bed." He slipped inside and gave me a little wave as he closed his front door.

I didn't waste time either. I dashed back to my house just long enough to grab my car keys. The storm was imminent now. Jagged flashes of lightning sliced across the sky and claps of thunder rolled off the lake one after another. It was almost eleven, not a reasonable hour to go visiting, but I'd fooled around along enough. It was time to tackle my own agenda.

On the trip down 9N, I reviewed the perfect scenario I'd planned for my reconciliation with Don. I'd intended to arrive at his house looking my best, dazzle him with a fabulous dinner, smooth out any bad feelings he might be harboring about the way I'd treated him at the Center and weaken any remaining defenses with his favorite red wine.

If this explicit come-on and its inevitable consequences didn't salvage our relationship, I'd even been prepared to apologize. Now only a very small part of the plan was doable.

At this point, I'd be bursting into his house, empty-handed, at a ridiculous hour, in a wildly disheveled state, with nothing more to offer than a sincere wish to get our relationship back on track. I navigated the turns on 9N with care, trying not to think about how I'd feel if Don didn't respond the way I hoped.

Even now with the summer gone, Canada Street in Lake George Village was lively, but the side streets leading to Don's place on the water were deserted. His house, like most of his neighbors' homes, was dark. What did I expect? Tourist season was over. The people who lived here had to get up and go to work. Don had probably gone to bed himself.

Even after I realized his car wasn't parked in his driveway, I didn't give up. I rang the doorbell again and again. When there was no response, I stumbled through the dark yard to knock on his bedroom window.

I'd banged on it several times when the storm hit with a vengeance. The rain swept off the lake in sheets, drenching everything in its path. Bolts of lightning seemed to crash all around me. I stood there in Don's yard for a few minutes more as the rain and wind pelted me. Then I ran for my car and drove home.

NINETEEN

THE NEXT MORNING I skipped my run and concentrated on drinking enough coffee to activate my sleep-deprived brain cells. My ridiculous behavior the night before and the hours of tossing and turning which followed had finally brought home to me how poorly I'd been handling my relationship with Don. In fact, saying I'd handled it poorly was a masterpiece of under-statement. I'd messed it up royally, and my attempt to straighten things out had gone tragically awry. So now what?

I'd poured my fourth cup of coffee and was starting around the same circuitous route I'd been traveling most of the night when someone knocked on the kitchen door. Not the best time for a guest. I'd showered but rather than make a decision on what to wear, I'd slipped back into my robe. My hair, still wet from the shower, hung tangled and uncombed; I hadn't applied make-up, hadn't even considered how much concealer I'd need to hide the black circles under my eyes.

I opened the door.

Don Morrison, the object of my concern, stood on

my doorstep, freshly showered, immaculately groomed and, judging from his scowl, not in the most agreeable of moods.

"Loren, what the hell is going on? I stayed in Albany overnight and my neighbor called me at the hotel at six o'clock this morning. He saw you wandering through my yard at midnight in the pouring rain and peeking in my bedroom window."

"Doesn't sound good when you put it that way, does it?" I forced a smile, but my attempt to be flip failed miserably.

Don continued to glower. "No, It doesn't. Will you please give me some hint as to what's going on?"

"Sit. Have coffee. Let me explain." Relieved to find coffee still left in the pot, I pulled a mug out of the cupboard and filled it for him. Then I busied myself finding cream and sugar and a Danish.

"Forget the stupid hostess bit," he growled. "Tell me what's wrong. What were you doing at my house so late?"

I did a quick rundown of the things I couldn't tell him. A guy I was crazy about for a long time dropped in last night. We had drinks and I served him the dinner I'd planned to bring to you. He kissed me, and I didn't object. In fact, I kissed him back. If I hadn't come to my senses, I'm not sure what else might have happened.

I couldn't say any of those things. So I did what any trapped rat would have done. I skipped over the part of the evening I wasn't proud of and shifted the blame to someone else.

"I'd planned to come earlier, but Arthur Blake asked me to help him look for his mother. That held me up." The explanation contained elements of truth, and I thought sounded reasonable.

But not to Don. "You did what? Arthur was looking for his mother? I understood she never left the house."

"She's started wandering around at night. Arthur was a wreck when he couldn't find her or the woman he's hired to look after her. We were about ready to start knocking on doors on Cove Road when he checked his house one more time and she was there."

"You mean she'd been there all along?"

"No. She had gone out but the caregiver was with her. She wasn't in any danger, but Arthur had no way of knowing that."

Don gave me another appraising look. "I still don't understand what this has to do with you peeking in my windows in the middle of the night. And why aren't you at work now? This isn't like you. What the hell's going on?"

I was about to acknowledge that Diane was right, that I was the low-life who threw the pearl away, except Don wouldn't have any idea what I was talking about and I was a little too weak on my Shakespeare to explain. I was saved from having to answer by fresh knocking on my kitchen door.

I opened it to find Millicent Halstead, in a highly distraught state, poised to launch herself into my kitchen.

As soon as I swung the door back, she did exactly that.

"Loren, I saw a face at my window last night. It was late. I was turning out the lights to go to bed. Then this shadowy form scuttled across the yard. It scared me to death. Did you see any sign of—?"

She stopped short. She'd been too caught up in her own concerns to notice Don, but in the next few seconds, she registered a scene she didn't expect. A male visitor, fully clothed, drinking coffee at my kitchen table early in the morning, while I, in what a generation or two ago would have called dishabille, lounged on a chair across from him.

"Sorry, I'm sorry," she gasped. "I…I didn't know you had company. I shouldn't have barged in on you."

Don didn't wait for an introduction. He shoved back his chair, jumped up and bolted for the door. "It's all right. I'm leaving anyway."

I followed him. "Don, wait. Are you headed back to Albany now? Please call me when you get there. We'll set something up for whenever you get home."

He gave me a look I couldn't read and slammed out.

Millicent, visibly distressed, collapsed into the chair Don had vacated. "Loren, I apologize. I didn't know you had a guest. I didn't notice a car."

I took a deep breath and changed the subject fast.

"Millicent, it's all right. I don't think your prowler is anything to worry about. Victoria Blake was wandering around last night. She was probably the person you saw."

Millicent winced as if I had struck her. "That's even worse. Why would she be in my yard? I've got friends coming to stay for a few days. I can't have Vicky Blake lurking around my house, looking in my windows."

"I'm not sure that's who it was, but maybe you could speak to Arthur, tell him you think she may have been in your yard last night."

"Oh, Loren, I couldn't do that. I don't know the man at all. Can't you talk to him for me? It would be so much better coming from you. I don't know what Vicky has told him about me." Her face twisted as if she might be starting to cry.

I didn't have time to kick the problem around, so I took the easy way out. "I've got to get to work, Millicent. I plan to stop at Arthur Blake's house on my way and make sure everything is all right. If Arthur's up, I'll tell him what you saw. I'm sure he doesn't want his mother prowling around your yard at night any more than you do."

Millicent thanked me over and over and proved her gratitude by leaving quickly. In a burst of confidence, I decided on a plan which I thought would get my life back on track. I'd dress fast, make sure everything was all right with Arthur and his mother, then head for the office. I'd resume my normal routine and later, when Don called, I'd start repairing the damage I'd done there.

The day had started off so poorly I thought things had to get better.

I was wrong.

TWENTY

WHEN I RANG THE BELL at the Blakes' house a half-hour later, Arthur cracked the door and peered out at me as if I'd interrupted something important. He was carrying an out-sized book, opened to a large, garishly colored photo of a vampire bat smeared with blood, and staring at it as if he couldn't tear his eyes away.

"Do you know if a vampire bat doesn't feed for two or three days it will starve, Loren? The bats, who have fed, share with it, and not just members of its family as some other species do, but unrelated bats. Isn't that amazing?"

"Amazing," I said, trying not to look at the bat's ugly little face. "I just wanted to make sure everything's all right here this morning."

"Of course. I shouldn't have alarmed you last night. Mother had gone out, but Darla was with her and she wasn't gone long. Nothing to be worried about after all."

I'd been involved in enough meetings where people reversed their stands on community matters to know the futility of disagreeing. Arthur had decided on this version of what had happened and he was going to stick to it.

"As long as your mother's okay—"

"She's fine." He pushed on the door.

I bristled. I didn't like having the door shoved at me. "Hold on a minute, Arthur. Millicent Halstead saw someone in her yard last night. Do you think your mother could have wandered up there?"

The remark ticked him off. His facial muscles tensed. His words flew at me in angry spurts. "I told you that woman's bad news, Loren. She's only here to talk people into buying her books. Then she'll be gone. She's a liar and a freeloader, that's what she is. Do you know vampire bats won't put up with freeloaders? They figure out what they're doing, and then they don't share with them. It says so right here." He banged a finger hard on one of the photos in his book.

"What makes you think Mrs. Halstead is like that, Arthur?" I made an effort to ask the question in a calm manner. I really wanted to know the answer.

"I've heard stories about her. She lived around here once before. Darla told me exactly where they went and it was nowhere near Millicent Halstead's place."

I gave up and turned away. "Fine. As long as you're okay with it."

Maybe I should have had more patience, I thought as I drove to work, but I didn't have time to argue. I'd passed along what Millicent had told me. If he didn't choose to believe me, there was nothing more I could do.

As it was, the morning was half gone by the time I reached my office. My first act, even before I made coffee—check for a blinking light on the phone. Nothing. If Don had called, he apparently hadn't left a message.

When the phone did ring a half hour later, I picked it up eagerly.

"Loren." It was Millicent Halstead's voice.

I tried not to sound disappointed.

"Do you remember I mentioned I had company coming? There's going to be a short service at the funeral home to honor Roberta's memory, then we'll gather here afterward. Just a few old friends who used to visit when Carl and I lived here at the lake. I've told them all about you and what a help you've been to me. This is the perfect chance for them to meet you."

I stumbled through an excuse.

"You don't have to stay all evening, Loren. Just say you'll pop in, even if it's only for a few minutes. Eight, or any time after. Whenever you can manage it."

I muttered something about having to let her know for sure, and that seemed to satisfy her. I could call with an excuse later. Or if Don didn't come back tonight, this might be my chance to meet some of those wild swingers the *Emerald Pointers* had referred to. Even my concerns about Don hadn't managed to stifle my curiosity about that crowd.

By two o'clock I'd accepted the fact that Don wasn't

going to call, at least while I was at the office, and I didn't think it wise to interrupt his meetings by calling his cell. I took time for a trip to the gym in the hope that exercise would smooth out my sharp edges, but even after an hour workout, I couldn't relax.

When I reached my house, I made a quick decision. Indian summer was hanging on and warm weather was back, at least temporarily. The lake was bathed in sunshine; the water sparkled as if it were a perfect summer afternoon. There might not be another day like this for a long time. A swim could be just what I needed to clear my head.

I slipped into a bathing suit, grabbed the biggest towel in my linen closet and hurried down to the water before I could come to my senses. This had been a day for making dumb decisions, and this made the cut as one of the dumbest. Wading in along the dock was sheer torture, relieved only when my extremities began to go numb. I swam to the end of the dock, circled around for a few minutes, then accepted the fact I was a coward and climbed out.

I'd started up the wide stone steps to the house when Stephanie Colvin, taking time from her afternoon shift at the *Post Standard,* hailed me from the lawn. She was lugging a packet of newspapers under one arm and making frantic gestures with the other as she hurried over to where I stood waiting.

"Loren!" she cried. "Have you seen the Albany

papers? All hell's breaking loose and you and your new buddy are right in the thick of things."

And I'd thought the day was going to get better.

"Come inside, Stephanie, or you'll be able to write a first person account of watching someone freeze to death in front of you. Give me one minute to get dressed and make coffee."

While I ran into the downstairs bathroom to dress, Stephanie sat down at the kitchen table and began spreading out the newspapers she was carrying. "You knew they identified the corpse you found, didn't you?" she called to me.

"Sure. Your paper ran the woman's name last week," I said when I joined her a few minutes later.

"But now there's more. This is what you call a new spin on it, I guess. I'm anxious to see what you think." She pointed at the papers she'd folded open.

I started a pot of coffee fast, then pulled another chair around and sat down at the table next to her.

Three Capitol District newspapers carried similar articles, all prominently placed with bold headlines, catchy subheads and accompanying photos. The accounts relied heavily on words like "skull," "skeleton," "murder," "corpse," "crypt," "grisly"…anything to sensationalize the story.

Among the names given prominence—Roberta Canfield (the dead woman, as identified by Sheriff's Investigator Jim Thompson), Millicent Halstead (an acquaintance from years back) and Loren Graham (the mayor of Emerald Point who'd found the skeleton).

"Jim is going to have my head," I told Stephanie. "This is so unfair. Darla Phillips is the one who found the skeleton, not me. She doesn't even rate a mention."

Stephanie gave me a rueful grin. "Maybe you should see this as a compliment. You're the mayor of this here burg. You stay on top of everything going on, even if you have to dig up a skeleton to prove it."

If she was trying to lift my spirits, she didn't succeed. "I didn't have to go into that cellar, you know. I get claustrophobic in places like that. Anybody with a grain of sense would have balked. Why didn't I?"

"Isn't it a little late to be asking that question now?" Stephanie said with a smile and went back to studying the articles.

The night before when I couldn't sleep, I'd finally quit making excuses for myself and accepted responsibility for the tension between Don and me. As for the discovery of the skeleton, I still considered myself an innocent victim of circumstances. Now I began to wonder if I wasn't guilty there too.

Stephanie skimmed through the articles one more time. "They've really scooped us bad. They've found out where the woman went to college and why she was here at the lake. We didn't have that information. Do you know any of this already?"

"Very little officially. But I picked up a few dirty

details on the goings-on when Millicent lived here with
Carl Durocher. She was married to him then, you
know."

"It says here the dead girl took a class from him
when he was a visiting professor in Albany," Stephanie
said.

I filled in a few blanks for her. "Rumor has it Millicent and Carl did some pretty wild partying here at the
lake, even included some of his students. This is way
back, before he hit the big time with his poetry."

"Is he still alive, do you know?"

"No. Died two years ago. I *Googled* him."

We were still mulling over the articles a few minutes
later when the phone rang.

"Loren." Don's voice, sounding very serious.

Not a good time for me to talk.

"We've run into more problems here. Bill Whitcomb
and I are going to have to go to New York, probably stay
there a couple of days to try to get things straightened
out."

"Won't you be coming home first?" My mind was
racing. He'd need clothes, wouldn't he? Even if he only
came home to pack, I could run down to his house.
Whatever was wrong between us was snowballing. I
wanted things straightened out.

"I've got clothes with me here. We're going to head
out right now," he said.

I hesitated, conscious that Stephanie was hearing

my side of the conversation. "I was hoping you'd be home tonight."

"So was I. But it can't be helped. I'll call you when I get back."

And that was that.

TWENTY-ONE

THE NEXT DAY the area was buffeted by a series of heavy storms, which left homes north of us without power and the residents of Emerald Point double-checking their generators and emergency supplies.

Darkness fell early. By six o'clock the lake was shrouded in gray fog, which oozed onto the docks and across the yards until it enveloped everything in its path. A perfect accompaniment to my dreary thoughts.

With no chance of getting together with Don, I decided to accept Millicent's invitation to meet her old friends. At eight when I left for her party, the fog had become even thicker and the houses on the bluff that were still visible had been transformed into ghostly apparitions in the gloom. This wasn't a night for walking up the hill. I took the car.

This time there were no luminarias lining the path to the front steps and no good-looking young men to welcome guests.

Millicent opened the door herself. "Loren, I'm so glad you came. We've just come in from the memorial service I arranged for Roberta. Everyone's looking forward to meeting you."

She led me over to a wheeled table in the living room—a tea wagon, my grandmother would have called it—and pointed to the assortment of wines she'd set out. I chose a Chardonnay, and she poured a glass and handed it to me.

As soon as I'd taken a sip, she stepped forward and signaled for attention from the dozen or so people standing or sitting in groups around the large room. "Listen up, everybody. This is Mayor Loren Graham. I'm so pleased she was able to join us."

She pointed to a couple with their heads together at the side of the room. "That's my agent over there, Trent Phelps and his assistant, Mary Lou Decker."

The two waved a greeting and went back to their discussion.

"And those folks on the couch were friends of Carl's. I'll make sure you meet them later."

We exchanged nods.

She took my arm and escorted me over to another group. "I want to start with these people, Loren, because they're especially anxious to meet you. They're old friends, Malcolm and Beverly Reynolds, and Christopher Cornwell."

The three of them stepped forward immediately to shake hands. They were probably all in their fifties, Millicent's age or older, trim, professional types in designer suits and New York haircuts, perhaps a little overdressed for a memorial service at the lake, but obviously accomplished at the meet-and-greet. They reminded me of dozens of people I'd met in the city.

Before we'd finished the first exchange of pleasantries, Beverly interrupted. "Loren, was it? Didn't Millicent say you were the one who found Roberta's body?"

I'd expected to be asked questions tonight, and I was willing to answer them if I could. But I intended my answers to be accurate. "No. Another woman in the neighborhood found her body. She came to my house and took me to the cellar to confirm the discovery. And it wasn't a body; it was a skeleton."

Christopher Cornwell edged closer. "But how long had it been there? It must have been there awhile if it was a skeleton. Have the police said how long?"

"Not police. The sheriff's department handles our law enforcement here," I explained. "They figure the body was in an empty cistern near the house for twenty-five years or more. When the cellar wall collapsed, it was swept along with the stones."

Christopher threw a sharp glance toward Malcolm Reynolds who stood staring at me, as if stricken dumb by my words. "This explains it, Mal. You finally know what happened to Bobbie. Face it. This answers your questions—why she never came back to school, why she never sent back your ring or got in touch with you."

"You knew her?" I asked Malcolm.

When he didn't answer, Beverly sidled closer to me. "This is very difficult for Mal. He and Bobbie had been going together. They quarreled, and she took off and came up here. He never heard from her again. Isn't that right, Mal?"

Malcolm nodded, still unable or unwilling to speak.

"So you knew she'd come to the lake but you never found out what happened to her?" I said.

Again, Beverly answered for him. "I suppose that's hard to believe now, but it was a different time back then. She'd stored a few clothes in an apartment she was going to share with three other girls the next semester, and left without telling them her plans."

"But didn't they think something might have happened to her?"

Beverly shrugged. "She didn't leave anything of value. Wasn't that what you said, Mal? They expected her back for the fall semester, but when she didn't show, the roommates figured she just took off. Maybe met a guy and went with him. That was the sort of thing she'd do."

Mal turned away and gulped several swallows of his wine.

"Didn't anyone contact her family or somebody here at the lake who might have known her?" I asked.

Beverly stiffened, apparently feeling I'd put her on the defensive. "Understand—I didn't know Bobbie or any of the girls she lived with. What do you think, Chris? You and Mal were roommates then, weren't you? Did anyone try to find her?"

"I guess. I mean, somebody must've tried to find her. I don't remember the details," Christopher said.

I didn't comment. I wasn't looking to blame anyone.

"Malcolm was terribly hurt, of course. Weren't you, Mal?" Beverly continued.

Another nod.

I directed one more question to Malcolm even though I suspected I wouldn't get an answer. "When did you realize she wasn't coming back?"

Again, Beverly jumped in. "It took a while, didn't it, hon? For him to believe she was really gone, I mean. I met him two years later and he was still obsessing about it. Kept thinking he might hear from her even then."

Was he really obsessing about Bobbie's disappearance or had there been something else in play? That's the trouble with having a suspicious nature like mine. I was picturing a whole different scenario. What if Mal had known very well what happened to Roberta Canfield—Bobbie, as she was called in those days— because he'd followed her to the lake, quarreled with her and killed her?

Two years later, still tortured with guilt, he'd met someone who not only believed in his innocence but also was willing to make his case to others. If you were inarticulate or afraid of incriminating yourself, a woman who did your talking for you would be a real find.

Before I could ask another question, Millicent in her role as good hostess swooped down on us. "Now, now. You people sound much too serious here. Let's freshen your drinks and lighten things up a bit."

Fine with me. As I followed her over to the wine cart, I took time to check out some of her other guests. Two women at the far end of the living room near the closed doors to the terrace looked familiar somehow. It took several covert glances before I realized I was seeing Julia, the woman I'd overheard lashing out at Millicent at the Lake George Club, and her sister. Strange, I thought, the woman had been furious at Millicent, and now she was comfortably ensconced in her living room, enjoying her hospitality.

When Millicent handed me my refill, I sauntered over and introduced myself. Julia's sister, the white-haired woman I'd seen her with at Millicent's talk, turned at once and extended her hand. "I'm so glad to meet you, Loren. Julia mentioned she'd seen you that day at the Club. I'm May Daniels."

Julia appeared calmer tonight, nowhere near as shaky as she'd been at the luncheon. She smiled up at me. "Nice to see you again, Loren."

"Julia was feeling a little under the weather that day. She told me you offered to help her," May said.

I nodded. I wouldn't have described Julia's confrontation with Millicent as feeling a little under the weather, but perhaps she hadn't told her sister the whole story.

"Millicent gave a fascinating talk at the Club, didn't she?" May continued. "Imagine her writing a book, not one book, but several of them. We thought of Carl as the author and Millicent—well, in those days she never seemed to get out of the kitchen. She was always slaving over those fabulous suppers Carl insisted they had to serve while he sat in the living room enjoying his cocktails, usually with an adoring audience of women hanging on his every word."

"Really?" I said. Again I felt a rush of sympathy for Millicent. What had her life been like? Had she really been little more than a servant to Carl?

"I didn't realize you'd known them in those days too, May," I said.

"Yes, I knew them both. But fortunately for me I didn't fall under Carl's spell the way so many others did." She glanced over at Julia but her sister offered no response.

Several minutes of silence proved too much for me.

"We had quite a storm that afternoon, didn't we?" I said finally, falling back on the universal safe topic— the weather. "And tonight we not only have rain, but fog. If you were hoping to see our fall foliage, Julia, you probably won't believe how many beautiful days we usually have this time of year."

Julia didn't reply but May picked up on my remark. "You're right. I tell her all the time how lovely it is here in the fall, and I'm not sure she believes me. My husband and I bought a place near Hague years ago, but this is the first time I've been able to get her to join us for a visit."

"Where are you from, Julia?" I asked.

I thought I'd asked a harmless question, but Julia didn't answer. Instead, she gazed past me, her eyes wide, her mouth hanging open as if she'd seen a ghost.

As I turned to look, I realized everyone in the room was staring in the same direction with expressions ranging from mild surprise to total disbelief.

They were all focused on the entrance from the hall where Millicent was escorting Victoria Blake into the living room.

TWENTY-TWO

I STARED TOO. I couldn't stop myself. Victoria Blake, her hand resting lightly on Millicent's arm, swept toward us like a visiting royal. And she was smiling. Not only was Victoria here, and here alone without Arthur or Darla in attendance, but what was even more surprising, she was smiling. The fact that she was coming into the room beaming happily made her appearance all the more shocking.

Tonight no one would have guessed she was in her seventies. She wore a soft silk dress perfect for her slender frame in a becoming shade of blue, and she'd done something extraordinary with her hair—or perhaps more accurately a very competent hairdresser had done something extraordinary with it. The color, which had been a pale shade of gray, was now an eye-catching silver. The waves were gone, replaced by a stylish cut with a few soft curls teased around her face. Even from a distance I could see she was wearing makeup, light touches of just the right amount of color, perfectly chosen and applied.

Julia clapped her hand to her mouth and turned to

her sister. "My God. Do you see who just walked in? Is this Mil's idea of a joke?"

"I don't think so," May said under her breath. "Look at her face. She's trying to hide it, but I think she's as shocked as everyone else."

Julia's hands shook. She staggered slightly, not as noticeably as she had at the Lake George Club, but enough that I stepped closer, thinking she might be going to fall. She reached out to seize her sister's hand.

"Julia, get hold of yourself," May muttered.

But Julia couldn't control her shaking. "I knew I shouldn't have come. I knew it. Why did I listen to you?"

As we stood watching, the two women reached the drink cart, but Victoria shook her head and continued past it. She was tugging Millicent after her now, rather than leaning on her for support, and she was zeroing in straight for the place where we were standing.

Julia made a soft moaning sound. Both she and May stared as if transfixed.

Victoria Blake didn't speak until she'd almost reached the three of us. Then she moved away from Millicent and extended both her arms as if to embrace Julia. "Julia, so good to see old friends again. How are you?"

Julia, apparently struck dumb, stood frozen in place.

Victoria wasn't deterred by her lack of response. She threw her arms around Julia and hugged her close.

"It's been a long time since I've been able to get together with friends from the old days. I've missed you."

Julia continued to stare, her face expressionless.

May came to the rescue. As soon as Victoria stepped back, she moved between the women. "I'm May Daniels, Julia's sister. Do you know Loren—?"

Victoria turned toward me. "Of course, I know Loren. She's our mayor and she's doing a wonderful job for our town. We all love her here."

That was news to me. The remark was definitely an improvement over her comments to me the last time I saw her, but I still thought it best to steer us toward a really safe topic. "Where's Arthur tonight, Victoria?" I asked.

She managed a little chuckle. "Oh Arthur's traipsing around up near Hague. Clem McTavish thinks vampire bats have been feeding on his cattle. It's very unusual to get a report like that around here, you know. There are only a few species of vampire bats worldwide. Arthur's so excited he's planning to spend tonight in the pasture. He's scared to death the bats will go into hibernation before he sees them."

And here I thought some of our Village Board members came up with creative excuses for missing a meeting. Maybe I'd try that one myself the next time I wanted a night off.

While I was casting around for an appropriate

comment, Millicent kept the conversation going. "You mean he's still interested in bats, Vicky? He wasn't much more than fifteen years old when I lived here before and even then, he was out on summer nights making his observations."

Victoria's smile disappeared. "At least there's one thing that doesn't change, no matter how much everything else does."

Where was Darla, I wondered? Did Victoria's sudden shift in mood mean that her new sociability was no more than a thin veneer? Was she really able to be here by herself? I glanced toward the entrance, hoping to see the caregiver rushing in.

No such luck. Victoria had apparently come to the party on her own and her former friends were going to have to deal with it.

To their credit, they made an all-out effort to do just that.

Millicent settled Victoria on a small loveseat and sat down next to her. The rest of our little group pulled up chairs and formed a half-circle around them.

May developed a sudden interest in bats of all kinds and posed a number of questions which Victoria, to my surprise—and probably to everyone else's—answered in depth. She'd obviously been listening to Arthur and was able to repeat some of his findings.

After a few minutes, Millicent found her voice again and commented on how well Victoria looked. "You don't seem to be aging, Vicky. You must tell us your secret. How are you managing that?"

Victoria, her dark mood of a few minutes before now gone, bestowed another round of smiles on the group. "I'm on a new medication and I feel like a different person. I can't tell you how much it means to enjoy life again."

"That's good to hear," Millicent said.

"Like the old days. We had so much fun that summer, didn't we?" Victoria directed the question at Millicent, then swung around to include Julia.

Millicent's expression froze. "Fun? Maybe some of it was fun, but…well, that was a long time ago."

Julia, her face a mask, didn't respond at all.

Despite the lack of encouragement, Victoria refused to quit. This time she focused her attention only on Millicent. "Speaking of the old days, how is Carl? You must hear news of him, even if you're not together any more."

Millicent continued to stare at her. Now she appeared even more dumbfounded. "Carl is dead, Vicky. You must have heard that."

It was Victoria's turn to be taken aback. "No. You don't mean it. Carl is dead?"

"I'm sure you must have read about it. It was in all the papers."

"I had no idea. What happened?"

"Heart attack is what I heard, but I don't know any details. None at all." Her tone made it clear there should be no more questions.

Victoria stared at her without responding.

Millicent reached over and patted her hand. "Vicky, let's not talk about sad things tonight. I want to hear more about Arthur's studies on the bats. I can't believe he's stayed with it all these years."

Still no comment from Victoria.

I was planning to come to Millicent's aid with a remark about Arthur's commitment to his research when I caught sight of something that stopped me cold.

As Victoria shifted in her chair, the loose-fitting sleeve of her dress fell back and for the first time I saw her watch. Or rather I saw a watch—an old-fashioned gold watch, its oval-face decorated with ornate scroll work and small decorative stones, with one stone missing—a watch I could have sworn was exactly like the one I'd seen hanging from the skeleton's arm in the cellar of Victoria Blake's old house.

TWENTY-THREE

As MILLICENT WAS STRUGGLING to redirect the conversation, the doorbell sounded a long, emphatic ring.

"I wonder who this can be so late," she cried as she jumped up and hurried toward the door. Her acting techniques definitely needed polishing

A minute later she led Darla Phillips across the living room to where we were sitting.

"Here you are, Victoria," Darla chirped. "I've been looking for you. It's time to call it a night, don't you think?"

"Darla, these people are old friends and they've just given me some very sad news. And we were having such a nice time catching up, weren't we?" She glanced around, as if asking for confirmation.

Millicent was the only one who managed a nod.

Victoria struggled to her feet and with Darla's help began picking her way across the living room toward the hall. Her movements were slower now, more uncertain, nothing like they'd been when she arrived.

As she and Darla reached the entrance to the hall, Will Broderick, who hadn't been present all evening, came charging out of the door which led to his apartment. He moved quickly across the room to stand next to Millicent.

"Are you all right?" he asked quietly.

She nodded.

When the front door finally closed behind Victoria and Darla, Millicent uttered a huge sigh of relief. "All right, everyone. Let's all have another drink. That was a surprise but we handled it very well, I think."

Not everyone seemed to agree. May was helping Julia across the room, supporting her as if she feared she might fall. Julia appeared distraught—in the same agitated state she'd been in that day at the luncheon.

May ignored Millicent and turned to Will. "Get our coats at once, young man. We have to leave."

Will, taken aback, started for the hall.

"Oh no. Please stay," Millicent insisted. "The worst is over now."

"The worst is never over with you, Mil," Julia whined, her voice trembling. "I shouldn't have come. I let May talk me into it and this is what happens. I wouldn't be surprised if you'd planned it this way."

"Of course I didn't plan this, Julia. I was just as shocked as you were when she walked in. She came here one other night. Do you think I would have come back to the lake if I'd known she'd invite herself over here whenever she felt like it? They told me she was an invalid—that she never left her house."

Julia struggled to make her an answer, but stumbled over the words.

May came to her rescue. "Julia's right. I should have listened to her. Nobody can believe a word you say, Mil. Once a liar, always a liar."

Before Millicent could reply, May grabbed two coats from the assortment Will had brought from the closet and helped Julia into one. She was putting on her own coat as she tugged her sister toward the door, leading her out in much the same way as she had done that day at the Lake George Club.

Despite Millicent's insistence that everyone else stay for another drink, the New York guests jumped up and insisted they had to call it a night as well. Millicent moved closer to me and grabbed my hand. "Don't you go, Loren. I have to talk to you."

"But—"

"Please. This has been so upsetting. I need you to stay."

The next few minutes raced by in a flurry of thanks and promises to stay in touch. Suddenly, the house was quiet. Millicent, still gripping my hand, drew me over to the couch.

"Sit a minute, Loren. Please. I need you here."

I'd have no luck protesting, I could see that. I sank down on the couch next to her.

To my surprise, Will chose a chair across from us. Whatever Millicent wanted to talk to me about, she wasn't keeping it secret from Will. Somehow he'd managed to get back in her good graces.

Millicent drained most of the wine from the glass she was holding before she spoke. "Loren, tell me. What's wrong with Vicky Blake? Do you know? People in town must have opinions about her but no one wants to share them with an outsider."

Was this why she'd wanted me to stay? I didn't have anything earthshaking to report. "As far as I know, Millicent, Victoria has been a recluse for years. You were right about that. But you heard her say her new medicine makes her feel better. Maybe that's why she's able to leave the house now."

"Nonsense. Can't you see it? She's on some kind of high. This is exactly the way she used to get—keyed up, very excitable. Then she'd crash. Carl made her worse. He'd single her out, pay her all kinds of attention. The minute he stopped…and he always stopped, that's the way he was. He could be so heartless sometimes." She shuddered as if the memory of Carl's behavior still caused her pain.

She'd brought up the subject. I had to ask. "Are you saying Victoria was involved with Carl?"

"Oh, yes. The man was a snake. He went after students usually. Vicky was something of a departure for him. We'd moved up here and she lived close by. She was very available. Made it all very convenient."

"Carl was involved with Victoria Blake?" I must

have sounded skeptical, because Millicent gave me an annoyed look.

"Yes, of course, Vicky Blake. Why would I lie about it? She was too old for him. He preferred teenagers like Bobbie and me, but Vicky was so willing, so desperate to be included. Sometimes he got a kick out of her, but then she'd become too clinging, too needy, and he'd start avoiding her."

I was having trouble fitting this together. "Are you saying he had an affair with Bobbie too? The dead woman?"

"A surprisingly long one for him. She'd also been a student of his. She was two years ahead of me. I knew her slightly at college. She'd been his favorite one whole semester—that was a record for Carl."

"And then he dropped her?"

"Dropped her for me. For a time, anyway." Two simple phrases, uttered in a cold, matter-of-fact way, but with so much left unsaid.

"But where did Victoria fit in?"

"Soon after we moved here. Let me think back a minute. He sandwiched Julia in about the same time. I don't want to leave her out. She was working at a restaurant in Lake George Village waiting tables. Very attractive. Lots of fun. Not a timid goose like she is now."

"Julia too?" Maybe those articles in the *Emerald Pointers* hadn't been such an exaggeration after all.

"Julia didn't last long. That's when he took up with Vicky. All he had to do was crook his finger and she'd come running. Drop one, find another. He was cruel that way. He knew he hurt people, but he didn't care."

"Victoria Grant. It hardly seems possible." Was this part of the reason Victoria had become a recluse?

Millicent ignored my comment and continued her account. "Then Bobbie followed us up here. Rented a room in town, started turning up at our house."

"And you were married to him then? You had to put up with all this?"

"Not at first. We had some good months. But once I lost the baby, Carl went back to his old ways. He always had opportunities. Women loved the tortured-poet mystique he cultivated."

"That must have been such a difficult time for you." I wanted to ask why she'd stuck around, why she'd put up with it, but I hesitated.

"Yes. It was very difficult, but I survived."

But Bobbie hadn't. Was that what she was implying?

I pressed for more information. "Those other people who were here tonight—how do they fit in? I understood them to say Malcolm Reynolds had been Bobbie's boyfriend?"

"The boyfriend she left behind when she followed Carl up here. When she disappeared, we assumed she'd gone back to him. It was a while before we found out differently."

Was Millicent telling the truth? Had the stories in the *Emerald Pointers* been accurate? Carl Durocher was ranked as one of the outstanding American poets of the last century, respected, idolized even. And this was what he'd been like? Still, he wouldn't be the first famous writer with a less than admirable past.

I found it hard to know what to say. "Millicent, I'm so sorry to hear this," was the best response I could come up with.

"It's difficult to think back to those days," she continued. "Apparently, I've underestimated how much I wanted to erase that time. I shouldn't have come back here. How in the world could I have thought it was a good idea?"

I wondered about the answer to that question myself. What had she been thinking of?

For that matter, what was I thinking of? I didn't need to be caught up in any of this. All I had to do was find out for sure that the watch Victoria Grant had been wearing tonight was in no way connected to the watch I'd seen on the skeleton's arm. Once I was satisfied it was coincidence, pure and simple, there'd be no reason for me to drive myself crazy with suspicions.

Simple enough.

TWENTY-FOUR

BUT, OF COURSE, it wasn't that simple. During the night as I struggled to find a comfortable position in bed, unable to stay asleep for any length of time, I couldn't stop thinking about the people who'd come to the lake for Roberta Canfield's memorial.

To begin with I didn't understand why Millicent had arranged the service and the reception afterwards, and arranged it without involving any of the dead woman's family.

She'd invited former friends of hers and Carl's to a place where they'd spent time together thirty years ago. Why? From what she'd told me, that time would have been best forgotten. If things weren't complicated enough, she'd added Bobbie's ex-boyfriend to the mix along with his wife and friend.

Many years ago, Millicent had taken Carl away from Bobbie and eventually lost him to her again, at least for a time. She'd seen Julia and Victoria—and, for all I knew, May as well—added to his list of conquests, then dumped. Could any of these women—Millicent included—have been angry enough with Bobbie Canfield to kill her?

I also wasn't willing to rule out Malcolm Reynolds, the boyfriend Bobbie had left behind to pursue Carl. I'd imagined a scenario where Malcolm had come to the lake, quarreled with Bobbie and killed her, but perhaps there'd been others who could have fit into that role equally well.

And if I was speculating, shouldn't I be including all the members of the crowd that the *Emerald Pointers* had written about in their gossip columns? Jack's father had apparently been one of them, and wouldn't there have been other men in the group too? After thirty years, was it even possible to know?

Bobbie had been struck with something hard, probably several times, then shoved into a cistern. Brute strength hadn't been necessary. A woman could have done that almost as easily as a man. And the murderer wouldn't have had to be someone staying at the lake for the entire summer, or even for an entire night. In fact, Bobbie's murderer could have killed her spontaneously in a matter of minutes.

Millicent believed none of the people who knew Bobbie realized she'd been murdered. Her murderer knew, of course. But as far as everyone else was concerned, Bobbie had simply disappeared.

The question which mystified me most, the question I couldn't answer was this: Why had these people come back now? Curiosity maybe, or genuine grief, or guilt? Perhaps to learn what evidence had been found? Or for closure maybe? Closure was a popular concept now. Maybe they wanted closure. No way could I know the answer to that question.

Something else too began slipping in and out of my consciousness just as I was finally falling asleep, something that had surprised me, but probably wasn't very important. I couldn't quite take hold of it. Then it came to me. Will, looking somehow less unkempt than usual tonight, had sat quietly across from us. He hadn't taken part in the conversation, but had apparently felt welcome to join us. Why the sudden shift there? Had he resolved his differences with Millicent? Had he been reestablished as her right-hand man? I couldn't know the answer to that either.

So I went back to the one thing I could know. Once I was sure Deputy Cronin had spotted the watch on the skeleton's arm in the same place I'd seen it, I could quit obsessing over Millicent and her friends. The watch— that was something I could find out about.

As soon as I finished at the office the next day, I headed for the Municipal Center, psyched for a spontaneous visit with Sheriff's Investigator Jim Thompson.

I found Jim's outer office empty and a scribbled note from Eileen, his secretary, saying she was running copies of a report in the machine room. I seized the moment and knocked on the investigator's door without being announced.

After he bellowed for me to come in, I took a few tentative steps into his office and stopped short. Jim sometimes looked even more formidable sitting down than he did when he was on his feet, and this was one of those days. I was treading on quicksand here and I knew it.

"Do you have time to answer one question?" I asked him.

He looked up from his papers. If there'd been a welcoming smile, I must have missed it. "You're not looking to start something, are you Mayor?"

"Not at all," I assured him, innocence personified.

"Good to hear." He pointed at the coffee maker with a questioning look.

"No coffee. Not trying to start something. Just one thing I'm curious about. When Darla Phillips dragged me over to the burned out house to see the skeleton, there was a wristwatch dangling off its arm. Now neither you nor Doc seems to be mentioning it. What's the story?"

"No story. No watch. Doc never saw one, Rick either."

"What?"

"No watch. Sorry."

"Jim, what are you saying? You're not implying I made this up, are you?"

"Mayor, I'm too smart for that. Don't you think I got a confirmation from the woman that went over there with you?" The exasperated half-smile meant he didn't expect an answer.

"So what are you saying?"

He sighed and settled back in his chair. "How can I make this clearer? I'm telling you neither Rick nor Doc ever saw a watch. If you did, it was somehow gone by the time Rick got there."

I was too startled for a minute to piece things together. Then I thought back to that night. After the deputy had responded to my call, he'd driven Darla and me over to the cellar, but we'd waited in the car when he went inside. "Maybe—"

"I know what you're going to say, Mayor, and I'm way ahead of you. You reported seeing a watch. Deputy Cronin didn't see one. That means—"

I did some fast addition. "That means somebody got in there between the time I saw the skeleton—it was around 10:30, I'd say—and maybe midnight when Darla and I went over there with Rick."

"You got it."

"But who?" *Should I mention Victoria Blake's watch?* Somehow this didn't seem like the right time to bring that up.

"Who do we think has been hanging out in that cellar? High school kids. Thought I told you that."

"You did."

"Probably made a good hangout by their standards, if only they hadn't busted through that wall and added an unwanted member to their club."

"Wait. Do you think one of them would take a watch

off a skeleton, Jim?" Was some high school kid that much gutsier than I was?

"Can't say. Rick's worked up a list and he's already talked to some of them. Nothing yet."

Nothing yet. That didn't mean Rick wouldn't turn up something eventually.

"So right now it's a dead end?" I said.

"For the time being anyway."

A dead end, was it? Maybe I could do something about that.

TWENTY-FIVE

THIS TIME MY PLAN to talk to Josie Donohue about the hideout didn't call for subtlety. I intended to ask some tough questions and press hard for the answers. Not that I expected to get them easily, but this nonsense had gone on long enough. Turning a burned-out cellar into a clubhouse might be harmless, even if I didn't like picturing what went on in there, but stealing a watch off a skeleton's arm was something else.

If I swung by the Donohue house around three o'clock, I might catch Josie for a private chat before her mother came home from the coffee shop. I'd probably find out more if I talked to her alone.

No matter how dreary my thoughts had been earlier that afternoon, the drive back to Emerald Point from the Municipal Center sent my spirits soaring. Autumn brought glorious days to this part of the world. The lakeshore, encircling miles of blue-gray water, pulsed with life. Both sides of the lake sported foliage in brilliant shades of orange and gold laced with enough patches of red vermilion and cool green to create a landscape of breathtaking beauty. The October sky, dotted with puffy, white cumulus clouds, added the year's loveliest azure blue to the mix.

I parked in Kate's driveway and waited. When Josie walked in from school ten minutes later, I followed her into the house. I didn't waste time.

"I hear Deputy Cronin is talking with kids who were hanging out in that cellar. Did you know that?" I said.

She shrugged. "I heard something."

"Has he talked to you?"

"No, but I know a couple of kids he asked about it. No big." She glanced away.

I could read her better now than I could when I first met her four years before. She was scared.

"Did you hear what questions he asked?"

"Yeah. Something about a watch."

I waited, always a good ploy with Josie.

"But Lor, nobody saw a watch. I think it's some kind of trick to scare us. I bet there wasn't any watch."

I hesitated, then spelled it out for her. "There was a watch, Josie. I saw it on the skeleton's arm when I went into the cellar, and it was gone two hours later when Deputy Cronin got there. Somebody must have gone in there and taken it."

"Ugh. You saw it. You mean somebody went in there and took it off the skeleton? Nobody I know would do something that crazy, Lor. That watch would have germs all over it, wouldn't it?"

"Good point. I really can't say for sure. What time

did this nobody see the skeleton without a watch on its arm?" I said.

She hesitated, unsure how much to tell me.

I waited again.

Finally, she made her decision. "All right. A couple of the guys heard a sheriff's car had been there around midnight. They went over before school the next morning to check things out and saw the yellow tape across the cellar entrance. You know the tape that says 'Do Not Cross'?

"They didn't think that meant them?"

"They figured the deputies meant to close up the place, so they sneaked in to get their stuff out."

"Stuff? Like what stuff?" I asked.

"Well, like a pick ax somebody brought in, and a crowbar. The guys had been trying to make the place a little bigger, that's all. So when they went in to get their tools out of there before the police found them, that's when they saw the wall had fallen in. There were stones scattered all over the place, I guess, and that skeleton you saw had come sliding right in with the stones. Gave them quite a scare, even if they tried to pretend it didn't. But they swear there was no watch. Honest, Lor."

"But somebody must have been there when the wall caved in," I said.

"Don't think so. Think they found it that way the next time they went in."

"Josie, come on."

"If there was somebody there when it fell, they aren't admitting to it."

"Maybe some other kids had gone in earlier?"

"They didn't. Those guys were the first."

"You believe them?"

"Sure. Why would they lie about it?"

If I'd wanted to take the time, I probably could have given her any number of reasons. But right then, I had other things on my mind.

TWENTY-SIX

AN HOUR AFTER I returned home from my visit to Josie, while I was still waiting for a phone call from Don, he came back.

He didn't ride up on a white charger the way romantic heroes are supposed to do—if you're still into that kind of thing—but putt-putted into the yard in his old Buick with the knock in the engine.

I opened the back door and stood waiting for him.

"I thought you were going to call," I said by way of greeting.

His reaction stunned me. "What? I failed to obey you? You told me to call and I didn't? That's the first thing we've got to talk about, Loren. You're too goddamn bossy."

"Me?" I said.

"Yes, you. I'm not your child or your employee or even a member of one of your friggin' committees. As a matter of fact, I don't know what the hell I am to you."

Sometimes it didn't take me long to build up a head of steam myself, and this was one of them. "So what am I supposed to do about that? Tell you in twenty-five words or less while we stand here in the doorway?"

"No, you're supposed to invite me in and—"

I stepped back.

He marched past me into the kitchen, yanked a chair away from the table and dropped down on it. The chair, hit hard with a two hundred pound weight, creaked in protest.

"Do you want—?"

"No. I don't want coffee or a drink or some goddamn sweet roll. I don't want you bustling around the kitchen giving me half your attention while you play hostess. I want to have a conversation with you. Sit down."

I'd never seen this side of Don. In fact, I'd seldom seen him even moderately angry. This was rage, nothing short of it, rage that turned his cheeks fiery pink above his dark beard and made the muscles in his neck go tight. I sat.

He stared at me without speaking.

"I take it things didn't go well in Albany," I said.

"Albany's got nothing to do with this. We're not going to talk about what I did in Albany." He slammed his hand on the table. "We're going to break down for once and talk about what place I'm supposed to have in your life. I've been wondering about that a lot lately. Then the other night at the center when the lights came on and I saw you standing there, winding up to smash me over the head with that stupid frog, I realized I had no idea how to answer that question."

My anger ebbed away, but a feeling cold as ice crept out from my mid-section into my extremities. I never liked to acknowledge fear, but sometimes it struck when I least expected it and didn't have time to fight it off.

"I thought I explained that," I said in the most reasonable tone I could manage. "I thought you were somebody sneaking in to rob the place."

"An unlikely event at any time and in a driving rainstorm, even less likely. But suppose I buy that, then answer this one. After the lights came on and you'd realized it was me, and you'd given up your idea of bashing me over the head with that ridiculous planter, why did you act like I was the last person in the world you wanted to see standing there?"

I started to protest.

"Don't waste both our time saying you didn't, Loren. Let's get this out in the open right now."

I had to give the guy credit. He'd zeroed in fast on the one question I couldn't answer. I hadn't been glad to see him. He'd been gone three weeks. I was anxious for him to come home—at least I thought I was. I'd pictured his homecoming: a leisurely, romantic dinner while we caught up, followed by some we've-been-apart-way-too-long lovemaking.

I had no idea what to say.

"Tell me the truth, Loren. You made me feel about as welcome as if I really was a burglar. Why?"

I shook my head. I couldn't find any words. Why

couldn't we have a drink or a cup of coffee while we talked? I shifted in my chair.

"No, don't get up. And no, I don't think this conversation would go better if we had a drink right now. I want to know exactly how you felt when you saw me in that doorway at the center."

He wasn't going to let me off the hook, I could see that. He rubbed his hands over his beard as if it burned him.

"Okay. I'll admit it. I wasn't glad to see you right then. Understand, an hour before or later, I would have been. I was a million miles away, caught up in what I was doing. And with the storm and then the lights going out, it was scary in there, I admit it, but I'm used to taking care of myself. I didn't need you to rescue me. And it was late—"

"No. Never mind tacking on the it-was-late excuse. You just gave me an honest answer, at least part of one. I know you don't need me to rescue you. I know you can take care of yourself. There's a lot in your world I don't share, and I understand that. Same way you don't share everything in mine. But that doesn't mean we can't have a life together."

I felt my throat tighten. I bobbed my head up and down.

"I realize you've been hurt, Loren. Hell, so was I. But we can't let that wall out what we could have together."

"You're right. I know you're right." I forced the words out. My throat was too constricted to say more.

Don waited, gave me time.

I tried again. It wasn't easy. "I'm sorry. It was a dumb way to react. I knew I hurt you, and then I couldn't find a way to tell you."

He still didn't say anything.

I fished through my pockets. I didn't even have a tissue.

Don pulled a paper napkin out of the holder next to him and handed it to me. "All right. We've got that much out on the table. Now maybe we can have that drink."

I started to get up, but he motioned me to stay in my chair.

"I'll do it. I know where you keep things. We've only covered the first half of our conversation. If you wanted a drink before, you'll definitely need one for part two."

He gave me a little half-smile as he bent down to grope in the low cupboard where I kept the wine. He pulled out a chardonnay we both liked, then took two of my best wine glasses out of the hutch.

"I've had my dinner, have you?" he asked as he filled the glasses and set them on the table in front of us.

I nodded.

"Good. Make sure this wine is what you want. I've got something even more important to talk about."

His anger had cooled a little, but his words still had an authoritative ring.

He waited until I'd taken a couple of sips of wine. "Loren, I think we've wasted enough time. I love you, and I want you to marry me."

I blinked. I thought I was going to tear up again. We'd relegated this subject to the basement two years before and slammed the door hard on it every time it threatened to make another appearance. Why was he bringing it up now?

"Marry you? Ten minutes ago you acted ready to clobber me. Isn't this a strange time to be talking marriage?"

"I agree. It's not only a strange time, but the circumstances are far from ideal. We should go away, stay in a fabulous resort somewhere, have a perfect weekend together and then decide to do it. But I'm afraid if I wait, you'll put those walls up again and it will be too late."

"Walls? I don't put up walls." I said.

Another flash of anger. "Loren, you're putting them up right now. You finally heard what I was saying a few minutes ago, but I can already sense you closing off. And I think I know why you do it. You're afraid you'll be hurt again."

"Thanks for the insight, but I don't need you to psychoanalyze me," I snapped, angry now myself.

"Sorry. I was going for a marriage proposal here, not an argument."

Apparently, I couldn't handle one without the other.

I took a deep breath and tried to calm down. "I admit I've got some hang-ups about marrying again. I thought I had a happy marriage. I was wrong. How do I know I won't make the same mistakes again?"

Don took his time answering. "I find the marriage idea a little scary myself, and I think you know that. The difference for me was I knew I was unhappy, figured Janet must be too, but we didn't talk about it, didn't try to fix anything. Maybe it couldn't have been fixed, but we didn't even try. That's a mistake I don't want to make another time."

Was that what he'd been doing tonight—trying to fix our mistakes? What would he say they were—that I acted too bossy, too independent, and that he'd been too agreeable, that he'd let me get away with too much? He didn't call me on anything very often, that was true. I'd seen a side of him tonight I hadn't even realized was there.

"Don, I don't know what to say. I do care for you very much. We have some great times together." I hesitated. "At least, when I'm not ticking you off. But how can we jump into marriage? We don't even know if we could handle living together."

"I don't want to be your live-in, Loren, if that's what you're talking about. Anyway, this is a pretty conservative place for the mayor to be shacking up with somebody. I say we bite the bullet—get married and make a life together before either of us gets any more set in our ways."

"That would give us until next week, I guess." I could sense the tension between us dissipating. We were slipping back into our usual good-natured banter. Maybe I could do this. Maybe I could commit to someone again.

Don reached for my hand. "I bet that could make the Guinness Book for most unromantic marriage proposal on record. Let's see if I can't put a little better spin on things," he said.

He walked around the table and gazed down at me with a warm, loving look. Six years before when I'd moved to Emerald Point after the break-up of my marriage, I didn't think anyone would ever look at me that way again. And now this kind, decent man wanted to make a life with me. Maybe he was right. Maybe it was time I stopped building walls and welcomed him into my world, not as an occasional drop-in, but as a husband.

I stood up and lifted my face to kiss him. He wrapped his arms around me, his body strong and solid against mine. His kiss was gentle at first, then more intense, more demanding, until I felt myself respond with my own desire for him. A rush of feeling swept through me.

"None of those girls in Hawaii could make me feel the way you do," he said when we came up for air.

"But you had to find out for sure?" I teased.

"You're wrong about that, Loren," he said, his expression serious again. "That's one thing I knew for sure a long time ago. But I didn't know what I could do about it."

And just when I came the closest I'd ever come to vanquishing my fears and telling Don Morrison I wanted to marry him, somebody banged hard on my kitchen door and shouted my name.

TWENTY-SEVEN

DON AND I GLANCED at each other with the same thought. Whoever it was, anybody knocking at my door at such an inopportune moment deserved the boot—and fast. Manners or no manners, this was not the time for unexpected guests.

I opened the door to find Arthur Blake, visibly distressed and ready to knock again.

"Loren, you've got to help me. It's Mother. She's disappeared. I'm beside myself." Sweat beaded across his forehead as he sucked in big gulps of air.

I'd been down this road before. I spoke in calm, reasonable tones. "Arthur, remember that's what you thought the other night and she was fine. Darla is probably with her again and they'll be back before you know it."

"No, you don't understand—"

He didn't have to explain further. Darla Phillips loomed in the doorway behind him. If Victoria had left the house, this time she'd done it on her own.

"I'm sorry. I'm sorry to do this. And you've got company again." Arthur glanced toward Don and gave a little start of surprise. When he'd asked for my help before, I'd been cozying up to Jack on the porch. Now it was Don standing with his arm around me. My reputation with Arthur was going down the tubes fast.

Darla stepped into the kitchen to echo his concern. "We're both really worried, Loren. She's been gone for several hours this time."

"Darla is supposed to keep tabs on her," Arthur growled, obviously anxious to cast blame.

Darla turned to Don and me to plead her case. "She tricked me. I see that now. All afternoon she kept telling me how tired she was. Then as soon as she finished her dinner, she insisted she wanted to go to bed. What she really wanted was to get away from me so she could sneak out of the house."

"You're being paid not to let that happen, Darla," Arthur said.

"I know. I know. It's getting to be more than I can handle. She's not rational. She's trying to trick me all the time. I can't out-guess her."

This was getting us nowhere. I jumped in. "Hang on a minute, you two. Arthur, when I saw your mother last night at Millicent Halstead's, she seemed fine. She certainly didn't act irrational then."

Arthur shook his head. "She was probably putting on an act there too. She does that some times. I'd gone up to the McTavish farm to watch for vampire bats—some very unusual sightings up there—and I'd left

Darla in charge. Mother got away from her then too."
He cast another disapproving glance at Darla.

"She did it almost the same way that night," Darla admitted, "pretended to go to bed and then sneaked out."

"You mean when you came after her at Millicent Halstead's house, you hadn't known where she was?"

"No. I'd been all over looking for her before I thought to go there."

Don, who'd been listening quietly to the conversation, stepped forward. "So we shouldn't waste any more time. Arthur, why don't you go home and call the sheriff's department? Ask them if they can send a car up here right away. Then, check through your house again, make sure she's not in there somewhere. The rest of us will divide up the neighborhood and go door to door. We'll start with Mrs. Halstead's place since that's where she went last time."

I added another suggestion. "Arthur, the night you and I were looking for her, she managed to get back into the house without our seeing her. Maybe you should wait at your house in case she comes home."

Arthur nodded and scurried off.

I found flashlights for the three of us, and we moved quietly out my back door and cut through the yard toward Cove Road.

"I'll search the backyards and outbuildings," Don said. "Why don't you girls each take one side of the road and go door to door?"

As Darla moved off ahead of us, Don pulled me aside. "You need a lot more work on accepting marriage proposals. I hope you realize that."

"I'm inexperienced. They don't come along often." I reached up and laid my hand against his cheek.

He tucked his hand over mine. "Later. We'll get Arthur's problem solved first. Then we'll see what we can do about ours."

As I watched Don strike off into the yard behind Millicent Halstead's house, a strange feeling washed over me. I remembered the figure I'd seen standing in that same yard the night of Millicent's party. Jim hadn't reacted well when I used the word skulking, but I still had no idea why that man had been lurking around. What if he was out here again tonight?

I'd already flashed on a number of things which might happen to Victoria if she continued to wander around alone at night—injuries in a fall, a tumble into the lake, disorientation that would leave her unable to find her way home. I hadn't considered the possibility that someone might actually do her harm. But that didn't mean it couldn't happen.

As Darla trotted off toward the Smiths' house on the opposite side of Cove Road, I rang the bell at Millicent Halstead's front door. Several minutes passed before an invisible hand pulled the door slowly open. Millicent, dressed for the night in a maroon velvet robe and sheepskin-lined slippers, peered around it.

"Loren, is something wrong? Why are you out so late?"

"Searching for Victoria Blake."

"Why? Is she wandering again?"

"Yes. She's gotten away from Darla. She hasn't come here tonight, has she?" I said.

"Come in, Loren. I'll tell you a couple things that might help."

I stepped into the hall but shook my head at her suggestion we go into the living room to sit down. "I've got to keep looking, Millicent. What did you want to tell me?".

"I didn't invite her here to that party. I want to be sure you understand that. She just appeared on my doorstep and insisted on joining us. Couldn't you see how shocked I was? I didn't have any choice but to bring her in."

"That's what Darla said. She'd been looking all over for her. And yet I thought she seemed fine. And she explained about her new medicine—"

"Of course. That's Vicky all over. She was always like that. Always ready with the explanation that made perfect sense—at least on the surface. Don't forget I've known her for a long time. She was obsessed with Carl, I told you that. I think the fact I came back here may have triggered some kind of reaction in her. She may even have thought he'd be coming here to join me."

"Is it possible she really didn't know Carl was dead?"

"I doubt it. But did you see the effect on her when I said he was?"

"I noticed she seemed very shocked." I could understand why Millicent was upset but I wondered again if her reaction to Victoria Blake wasn't a bit overblown.

"I get a feeling you think I'm exaggerating, but Will can tell you…" She glanced toward Will who'd appeared in the hall behind us.

Will apparently slept in clothes even more disreputable looking than his usual daytime attire—a shabby, extra-large, gray cotton tee and navy gym shorts which exposed an unsettling expanse of hairy legs. My theory about his improved appearance went down the tubes fast.

"I heard the bell, then voices. What's going on?" he said.

I tried to avoid looking at him as I gave him a brief rundown.

"Vicky Blake is a very strange character, Loren," he said when I finished. "She seems weak, but she won't quit. She's gone out of her way to spoil things here for Millicent. I wouldn't be surprised if she's trying to force her to leave."

I glanced quickly over at Millicent, expecting her to insist she would never give Victoria Blake that much power over her.

To my surprise she agreed with Will. "He's right. I can't stay around and put up with her nonsense. Please don't mention this to anyone else but I've made a call to my Realtor. She had a couple of other people interested in this house and it may not be too late to make a deal with one of them."

Not much sympathy for Victoria in that house, I thought as I went on to ask questions at the other houses nearby.

Some of the other neighbors showed more concern but none of them had any idea where she might be. By the time I reached the end of the road and the cellar of the burned-out house, I'd lost track of Darla, but I could see red lights flashing below me on the shore of the lake. Two sheriff's cars had parked on a strip of sand and several men in uniform were pacing back and forth, shining lights out over the water.

That was the possibility I hadn't wanted to think about. What if Victoria had wandered into the lake or even fallen in somehow? We were running out of places to look.

I was starting to make my way down the hill to the shore when I had another thought. Probably a far-fetched idea, but what if Victoria had somehow gone into the cellar of the burned-out house? She'd lived in that house, after all. She'd probably heard talk about a skeleton being found there. It didn't sound like anything the average person would do, but Victoria's actions were not predictable.

On impulse, I backtracked up the hill to the cellar. I definitely didn't want to go inside that awful place again, but at least I could shine my flashlight down into it.

The sharp rocks that lined the entranceway to the cellar were streaked with mud after the recent rainstorms. As I stood there trying to decide if I was brave enough to slide down even part way into that yawning chasm, I heard a faint voice. "Who's there? Why are you shining that light in here?"

I made up my mind fast. I stuck the flashlight inside my jacket, pulled it tight around me and sidled down the same rocky aperture I'd crept down with Darla the night I saw the skeleton.

Victoria Blake, clutching the electric lantern Darla and I had found there that night, huddled on the disreputable old couch the teenagers had brought in for their clubhouse. Her clothes were caked with wet mud.

"Victoria, are you all right?"

Then because I never know enough to ask one question and wait for the answer before moving on to the next, I asked her why she was there and what she was doing and if she didn't think it was time to go home.

"Who are you? What are you doing in my house?" was her only reply.

I dropped the questioning and explained who I was. When she didn't respond, I added that it was much too cold for her to spend any more time there. I was debating whether I should try to get her out of there by myself or leave her and run for help, when she surprised me.

"You're right. It is cold." Her teeth were chattering.

"You need to get home right away, Victoria. Arthur's very worried about you. You've been gone a long time."

"I wanted to make sure that Bobbie wasn't still hanging around here," she said.

"Bobbie?" I asked.

"That tramp, Bobbie. She meets Carl here sometimes, you know. Wants to steal him from me. I can't keep her away from him."

"But she's not here now, is she?" Reassurance was obviously called for, even if what she was saying sent cold shivers down my spine.

"No, and she won't be. She won't be here any more now."

Victoria stood up. I reached for the lantern and gently unloosened her fingers.

"Can you walk, Victoria?" I asked.

"I can walk fine, just as good as anyone else," she snapped.

We picked our way across the cellar, almost inch by inch. When we reached the narrow incline that led outside, I thought it would be safer to let her go first.

"Duck your head and start climbing up, Victoria. We'll take this slow and easy."

I propped my shoulder against her back and tried to guide her with one hand on her waist. With the other hand, I held the lantern high enough to cast light on the treacherous footing ahead of her.

We moved slowly, one difficult step after another with long pauses in between.

"You're getting in my way, Bobbie," she growled as we neared the top of the incline. She squirmed, trying to pull away from me.

I took a half step back. "Victoria, it's me, Loren, your neighbor."

"No one wants you here. Carl doesn't want you."

"Yes, I know that." I tried for a reassuring tone. I was still standing close enough that she could feel my shoulder behind her. I slid a little farther away from her, attempted to give her more space even though I was afraid she could fall.

I poked my foot around, searching for a level spot, trying to find a firm place to stand, when she swung her body toward me. Her eyes in the light of the flash burned with hatred. "I told you to go away, Bobbie. Why didn't you do it?"

She cocked her elbow and threw a hard jab into my midsection. The blow caught me off guard, made me stagger sideways. One foot landed on a mean hunk of rock and turned over; the other sank into wet sand. She punched me in the gut a second time and before I could catch myself, I was tumbling backwards, slip-sliding head first down the narrow shaft as the lantern took off on its own and sailed out of reach. And before I could break my fall or even reach out a hand to protect myself, Victoria landed on top of me.

We lay there, both unable to move. After a minute I gritted my teeth and slid out from under her as carefully as I could. As soon as I could manage another move, I shoved myself along the cellar floor until I reached the lantern that—miraculously—was still working.

I lifted it gingerly and shoved myself back toward Victoria. "Are you hurt?" I asked.

"No. I don't think so. Are you?" She reached for one of the rocks in the entranceway and began pulling herself to her feet.

Her concern for me was the first sign she was back in the present. She seemed clearer—I was relieved to notice that—but it was too soon to answer her question. I tried some gentle movements on my arms and legs to see if they were willing to cooperate.

My right knee let out a shriek of pain. I reached down a hand and felt around the kneecap. I couldn't feel any cracks or outcroppings of bone, but something along the side of my knee was already throbbing painfully. Tendon? Ligament? I couldn't tell. But it needed attention and the sooner the better.

It was too late now to wish I'd gone for help when I found Victoria, so I had no choice but to introduce Plan B. As soon as Victoria appeared able to crawl up through the narrow exit, I urged her to start climbing. She complied willingly enough, without a backward glance. Once she'd started up, I inched along a few feet behind her to aim the light ahead of her as accurately as I could.

I had to give Victoria credit. She was in her seventies, and she'd taken a bad fall. Granted I'd served as a cushion, but she'd hit hard. She worked her way up the passageway, not fast but without any setbacks, until she slithered out onto the ground outside.

I gritted my teeth and followed, pulling with my hands and digging in with my right foot to lever myself up while my injured left leg dragged helplessly behind me. By this time we were both covered with mud. The dark gray sweat suit Victoria was wearing was caked with it; even the hood hanging down her back was soaked.

Once outside, I crawled to an open place in the trees and waved the flashlight around. The deputies responded quickly, charging up the hill at top speed, and then calling Arthur and Don on their cell phones to tell them the news.

This would have been the perfect happy ending if it hadn't been for the throbbing pain in my knee and the gnawing feeling in my gut about the things Victoria had said.

TWENTY-EIGHT

A SHORT TIME LATER, I lay propped on the couch in my living room while Don raided the freezer to make cold packs for my knee and Rick Cronin and another deputy milled around as if reluctant to tear themselves away.

I called Rick over to me. "I have to tell you this, Rick. Something very eerie happened in the cellar. I'm not sure how to explain it, but I think Victoria thought I was that woman whose skeleton was in the cistern. She called me Bobbie and told me Carl didn't want me here. She sounded as if she hated me."

"Tell me exactly what she said." Rick pulled his notebook out of his pocket.

I repeated Victoria's words. "She said, 'No one wants you here. Carl doesn't want you here. I told you to go away, Bobbie. Why didn't you do it?'"

Rick wrote the words down carefully in his little book and then read them back. "Are you sure those were her exact words? It does sound as if she thought you were somebody else."

"Yes, and then she elbowed me hard to shove me away from her."

I considered telling him she'd actually done more than elbow me, that she'd deliberately pushed me and pushed me hard when we were climbing out of the cellar, but something held me back. It was one thing to reveal that Victoria was confused, another to claim she'd turned around and shoved me down that entranceway on purpose.

"Wait. Are you saying she was babbling or that she meant to push you?"

I described her movements again and repeated everything she'd said, but I didn't elaborate. Now in my lighted living room with others nearby, her ramblings didn't seem as alarming as they had in the cellar.

"Could she have just lost her balance?" Rick persisted.

"She elbowed me hard. I'm sure of that much. This will sound strange, Rick, but I had a really odd feeling when she said those things—almost as if she'd gone back in time and was talking to the woman in the cistern."

Rick's eyes opened wide, but he didn't comment. "Investigator Thompson will be here first thing in the morning. He'll have my report by then but be sure you tell him everything you told me."

"Maybe you could break it to him first, Rick." I wasn't looking forward to a debriefing from Jim.

"I'll have my report on his desk when he comes in, but he'll definitely want to hear it from you too."

"Of course. Why did I think I could avoid it?"

"In the meantime, Mayor, I'll caution Arthur about keeping a close watch on his mother. She can't be wandering around at night like this. If that woman he hired can't handle her, he'll have to find somebody who can or keep a closer watch on her himself." Rick scribbled another half page of notes in his little book.

"Rick, you've covered all the bases. Why don't you call it a day?" I said.

He checked back through his notebook. "I want to be sure I have this right. The investigator will be really upset when he finds out you were hurt."

"I doubt he'll stay upset long if he can find a way to blame me for everything that happened," I said. "Keep telling him none of this was my fault and try to make him believe you."

Rick finally tore himself away and Don, a former EMT, took over with another ice pack and pain pills he found in the medicine cabinet. When his final attempt to get me to go to the hospital for x-rays failed, he wrapped my knee in an ACE bandage.

"If this doesn't help, I'll take you to see a doctor first thing in the morning," he said.

Things were finally quieting down when Josie Donohue, whose Early Warning System had some-how alerted her to my accident, arrived breathless with excitement.

"I've already asked my mother and she says I can stay here tonight and take care of you, Lor."

Don and I exchanged glances as our last hope for time alone together disappeared.

He shrugged and nodded toward Josie. "Looks like you're in capable hands for the night. Why don't I help you up to your room—you'll sleep better in your own bed. Josie can stay down here on the couch and check on you once in a while in case you need more pain medicine."

"Not exactly the homecoming I wanted with you," I told him when Josie had dashed upstairs to turn down my bed.

He smiled. "It's all right. This is her chance to do something for you and she wants to help. I'll take a rain check for whenever your knee stops hurting."

"I'll make it up to you," I promised as I eased myself into a sitting position on the edge of the couch and struggled to get to my feet.

"I'll be counting on it," he said. Then, when he saw me wince as I put weight on my left foot, he picked me up and carried me up the stairs.

As soon as Don had settled me on the bed, he turned to Josie. "I'll bring breakfast for you both. And Loren, you may want me to take you for that X-ray. You can see how the night goes before you decide."

Don said his goodbyes, and with Josie's help I slipped out of my clothes and pulled a loose-fitting nightgown over my head. My eyes drooped. The pain pills had already started their work when Josie tucked a blanket around me and went downstairs.

I couldn't tell how long I'd been asleep when I

heard footsteps on the stairs. "Josie?" I called, but there was no answer.

I had no idea how much time had gone by since I went to bed. I couldn't see the alarm clock on the dresser across the room. All I knew was that the pain in my knee had ratcheted up to an almost unbearable level.

Trapped in a nether world between dozing and waking, I heard Josie slip silently into the room. "Josie…"

But even as I said her name, I knew the dark shape looming above my bed wasn't Josie.

Before I could cry out, I saw a flash of movement. A white rectangle swooped down and smashed against my face, covering my nose and mouth. I couldn't breathe. Fighting for air, I tried to force my head to one side, but I couldn't move it. The pillow was pinned to my face, held there by powerful arms. No matter how hard I strained, there was no way to turn my head, no way to suck air into my lungs.

Frantic, I grabbed at the fingers, trying to dig my nails into flesh, but the hands were encased in some kind of thick gloves. I reached upward for the arms, hoping to feel flesh I could pinch or scratch. My fingers slipped along the sleeves of something smooth, some kind of nylon jacket. I wrapped my fingers around the wrist-band and gave a sharp tug. A piece of cloth tore free but the hands didn't loosen their pressure on the pillow.

I swung one of my arms back, grabbing for anything on the nightstand I could use as a weapon, but there was nothing within reach.

My left knee felt as if someone were holding a blowtorch to it, but the need for air drove me. I kicked wildly with both legs, but my attacker stayed above and behind me where I couldn't make contact. I could only reach the arms and they were too strong for me to move. I felt consciousness slipping away.

In a last desperate effort, I brought my knees to my chest, lifted myself as far as I could off the bed and thrust my legs up and back with all my strength. I heard a startled grunt as my left foot connected with something solid. Pain from my knee raced along my nerves, setting my whole body on fire. A dark penumbra encircled everything, whirling around dancing flames, but I felt the weight on the pillow lessen. I got one hand under it and pushed it away from my face and gulped big sobbing breaths of air.

I felt my attacker move away from the bed, heard the clatter of footsteps on the stairs, but I didn't dare hope he'd given up. What if he came back with a weapon? And what about Josie downstairs on the couch? Had he seen her there and done something to her before he came upstairs?

I swung my good leg out of bed and planted it firmly on the floor before I tried to put any weight on the injured one. As much as my knee had hurt before, the pain now was infinitely worse. Why couldn't I have made contact with my other foot?

I reached for the dresser and dragged myself along it until I could take hold of the door casing, then lunged for the little chest at the top of the stairs. As I hitched along, I turned on every light switch I came to. When I got to the stairs, I sat down and slid from step to step with my left leg held out stiff as a hunk of wood in front of me.

"Josie," I shouted as I reached the lower hallway. I called up every ounce of strength I could muster and struggled into the living room. I seized hold of the edge of the door and clung to it as I peered into the darkness, scanning the shadows for signs of the intruder. An eerie quiet prevailed. I felt for the wall switch and turned on the overhead light. I held my breath, terrified of what I would find.

Josie was gone.

TWENTY-NINE

"JOSIE, WHERE ARE YOU."

I hobbled through the dining room, calling her name, reaching for the back of one chair and then another to support myself. I shoved open the door to the downstairs bathroom. No sign of her. I grabbed the cotton cover-up I kept there to throw on over my bathing suit and put it on. It wasn't six o'clock yet and barely daylight, but maybe she'd gone outside. I headed for the back door.

As I dragged myself into the kitchen, I heard a rustle of movement behind me. Before I could turn around, something hard slammed against my head. I felt a great explosion of pain in my skull, sensed that I was reeling out of control and falling, and then nothing.

The next thing I knew I was struggling up a long tunnel. I came back to consciousness slowly, clawing my way up out of a dark space, a black hole without light or air. My head pounded. For a few seconds I thought I was pulling myself up out of the cellar of the burned-out house. But as my mind cleared, I knew I wasn't back in that cellar.

Somehow I was hurtling through space. Everything around me was moving at a furious clip. Several minutes passed before I realized I was in a vehicle of some kind, in the back of a truck or maybe a car with its rear seat taken out. It was dark. I couldn't see anything. Something scratchy covered my face.

I tried to raise my hands to pull it off, but they were immobilized. I could feel ropes or cords holding them together behind my back. The more I struggled, the tighter those bonds held me.

I felt myself starting to panic. I couldn't let that happen. I concentrated on taking a half-dozen slow, deep breaths. The ache in my head seemed unbearable, but as I shifted my body, I became conscious of even more searing pain in my knee. I remembered a fall. I'd hurt that knee when I tumbled back into the cellar of the burned house and Victoria had come crashing down on top of me.

But that wasn't all. Something else had happened. I fought to remember what it was. Something—no, someone—had been smothering me. I'd used that same leg when I kicked at the intruder, drove it into whoever was holding the pillow on my face, willing to do anything I could in order to breathe again. The pain in that knee had been agonizing from the first, but now my whole leg was on fire. I thought of the pain pills on my bedside table. They were no help to me now.

This had to be a nightmare, except I knew I wasn't asleep. I struggled to escape into a half-baked form of meditation a friend had told me about. It didn't work. In desperation, I began counting slowly backward from one hundred, taking even longer, deeper breaths, trying to relax my mind and body enough so I could slip under the pain.

Maybe I was still groggy from the blow to the head because I felt as if I dozed again. The next thing I knew a car door creaked open. I was lifted out. Strong arms carried me down a slope into a dank, stale-smelling room. I didn't think I was in the cellar this time, at least not the same one. Even with my face covered. I was aware of a different smell, along with a frightening re-alization that we'd entered a dark place. No light at all penetrated the cloth over my head.

After what seemed an eternity, I was set down—not on a couch or chair, but on cold, rough ground. The material over my head had twisted; it pulled tight against my nose and mouth, cutting off air, suffocating me the way the pillow had done a short time before.

"Help me. I can't breathe," I gasped and began to choke.

Mercifully, hands loosened the hood, or whatever it was, covering my face. Then in a quick movement it was torn off, and I was yanked into a sitting position against a wall. Arthur Blake bent over me, his lined face expressionless in the light from an electric lantern hanging on a nearby hook.

We were in another cellar, or was it a cave? My eyes

darted around trying to pick out openings, landmarks, anything which would tell me where I was. I needed a few minutes for things to start falling into place. I got the sense of an underground room of some kind, not a cellar, maybe a mine, maybe the mine where Arthur counted the bats. I'd heard people talk about it, but I'd never seen it myself—an old graphite mine, one of several in the area, abandoned long ago.

Why would Arthur have brought me here, to this closed, dark place? This couldn't be happening. There had to be some logical explanation. But as my eyes adjusted to the light, I saw something which confirmed my worst fears—a jagged hunk of cloth missing from one of the cuffs of Arthur's jacket, a piece the size and shape of the nylon I'd been hanging onto as I stumbled out of my bedroom after the intruder. That torn cuff confirmed what I knew, but hadn't wanted to believe—Arthur Blake, my longtime neighbor and—I thought—friend, had tried to kill me earlier tonight and now had brought me here, maybe intending to finish the job.

A gust of warm air from somewhere deep inside the mine swept over me. The dank, musty smell brought back the stench of the basement of the burned house. As eerie shadows played over the walls and crept toward the roof almost twenty feet overhead, I could see glittery specks sparkling in the dark stones. Could Arthur have brought me to a more frightening place?

I kept looking upward, wondering if hordes of bats were going to descend on me.

After a minute or so, I pulled myself together enough to ask some of the questions whirling around in my brain. "Arthur, why are you doing this? Where is Josie Donohue? Did you do something to her?" Getting those few words out started my head throbbing even more.

Arthur didn't answer my questions. He'd sunk down on the dirt floor of the mine a few feet from me. He was sweating and breathing heavily, his rasping intakes of air even louder than my own. "You hurt me, Loren. You kicked me right in the gut. I've got an ulcer. You probably started me bleeding."

The man had attacked me, tried to smother me to death, brought me to this terrible place, and he was complaining that I'd kicked him? I couldn't believe it. I started to tell him I was glad I'd hurt him, that I wished I could have hurt him even more, but I caught myself in time. I choked back the words. Desperate times called for desperate measures. No matter how dumb I felt doing it, it might be better to play along, to try to stay in our old neighborly relationship.

"Arthur," I said. "I'm sorry. I never wanted to hurt you, but you were suffocating me. It was self defense."

"I don't care, Loren. You still shouldn't have kicked me like that," he whimpered. He managed to get to his feet, but then began hugging his midsection as he rocked back and forth.

This was getting me nowhere. I had to know about Josie. "Arthur, what did you do with Josie Donohue?"

"Never mind what I did about her. Worry about yourself."

"But if she knew you came after me, Arthur, she'll tell the deputies. They'll be looking for you to find out what happened to me."

He gave me a disgusted look. "People call me slow—I've heard 'em—but I wouldn't do something that dumb. Don't worry about it." He began to cough again, deep barky coughs that reverberated off the walls of the mine. "Anyway, they'll be looking for you in the lake, you can bet on that."

"In the lake? Arthur, that's crazy."

"Like you didn't go in just the other day? I saw you splashing around out there like a crazy woman. You're in the water every chance you get. I know you got out and went in the house when your friend came, but she knew you'd been swimming." Another spasm of coughing doubled him over.

Had Arthur been watching me, keeping tabs on what I did? And what had he done with Josie? This was getting crazier by the minute. If he planned to keep me here—or worse—he'd have to come up with a better way to explain where I'd gone.

"But Arthur, nobody's going to think I went for a swim in the middle of the night."

He gave me a disgusted look. "They won't think

you went for a swim during the night. It'll be daytime before they know to start looking for you. They'll see your towel and shoes down on the dock where I put 'em and they'll think you went for one of your early swims. I'm not stupid, you know."

I'd really upset him now. I could tell from the way he gasped and rattled. His voice was growing weaker. Maybe he was right; maybe he was bleeding internally. If he passed out here in the mine, I'd be helpless. With my hands and feet bound tight, I'd be left to die right here.

I had to think of something I could do. I shifted my head a little, straining to look further back along the mineshaft. Another passageway, supported by wooden posts and lighted by a string of bare bulbs high on the wall, led off from the space where Arthur had put me down. Piles of broken and twisted rails were heaped near the entrance. A rusted wheel, possibly from a rail car, leaned against a beam

He'd seemed to appreciate the sympathy I'd offered earlier, so I tried more. "Arthur, you sound terrible. Are you all right? Maybe you need a doctor."

"No. I'm not all right." He groaned again.

"I don't think you sound so good. Maybe you should go to the Health Center."

I was hoping to reinforce the idea something was wrong with him, that he needed to see a doctor and that I'd help him in any way I could, but he suddenly switched gears and began ranting about me and how I was the one responsible for his problems.

"I didn't want to do this, Loren, but people are right about you. You meddle. You're a busybody. That deputy told me what Mother said to you. You know Mother's not clear sometimes, but you couldn't let it go. You had to tell him. He came right to the house last night after he left you and asked questions, said he'd have to report what you told him to the sheriff."

Was that the reason for all this? Had my comments to Rick Cronin triggered this response? I'd thought I was holding back a lot of what happened in the cellar. Had the little bit I did say started this landslide?

"But, Arthur, I'm sure I didn't tell him anything you should worry about. Rick probably told you just enough to upset you. Everyone knows your mother isn't always clear about what she means." I tried to remember exactly what I'd said to Rick. Maybe I could whitewash those comments, make Arthur see them in a better light.

"She may not always be sharp these days, but Mother's clear enough about what happened to that girl. She shoved her in that cistern and she remembers doing it."

I stared at him, as I fumbled for words. "Wait. Are you talking about the skeleton? Arthur, your mother gets confused, doesn't she? She probably didn't have anything to do with that."

He shook his head. He spoke slowly, his voice low

and serious. "I saw her do it, Loren, saw her hit that girl hard with a board two or three times and push her into the cistern. It was a long time ago—I was only fourteen—but I'll never forget it. I put the cover back on, and we never told anyone. But now she's told you. You're the only one besides me who knows for sure."

"You saw that girl in the cistern and put the cover back on, Arthur? How could you be certain she was dead?" I pictured the scene, horrified by what might have happened.

He glared at me.

I'd said the wrong thing again, made him angry.

"She was dead all right," he insisted. "You're such a damn bleeding heart. It's like you to worry about that."

Waves of nausea swept over me. It was hard to tell if they came from my horror at Roberta Canfield's fate or fear about my own or the pain coursing through me.

I tried to pull myself together. I needed to reassure him. "Arthur, nothing can happen to your mother now. Too much time has gone by."

"You're wrong about that, Loren. They'd put her away in a home some place. That's what she fears the most. I can't let that happen to her."

"Wait. Stop and think. You don't want to make things worse. I can help you figure out what to do."

He wasn't hearing me. "I've kept Mother safe all these years. My father didn't, you know. He left us in a terrible fix. Gambled everything away, lost all the money from his business."

"Your father did that? I didn't know." I'd heard the stories, but I'd never known anything for sure. My mind was racing. I had to think of something.

"Mother and I had nothing. Your grandfather took our house. Did you know that? He'd loaned my father money, and when he couldn't pay, he took the house. He was heartless about things like that. Served him right the house burned down right after he got it. He had the nerve to say Mother set the fire. Maybe she did. I wondered about it myself, but nobody could prove anything."

"Arthur, I didn't know. I didn't have any idea." Was he right? Was this one of the things people had held against my grandfather? It sounded as if Victoria Blake had found a way to get even with him.

"My father moved us out of our big house into that little cottage where we live now. Then he killed himself. All Mother and I had after that was each other. I've always taken care of her."

"People know that, Arthur. You have everyone's respect for the way you've done that."

I wasn't trying to flatter or manipulate him. I'd spoken the truth and I could see he was pleased by what I'd said.

He began to tell me more. "It's gotten so much harder lately since Mother's been wandering. That's why I hired Darla, but she hasn't done a very good job."

"Wandering? Was that what she was doing that night I helped you look for her?"

"She'd slipped away from Darla that night. Darla wasn't careful enough. I told her to hide Mother's clothes. She did it, but then she didn't notice when Mother started sneaking into my room and taking mine."

Something clicked in my brain. I'd thought Victoria had been wearing men's clothes the night I'd found her in the cellar of her old house. The figure I'd seen on the bluff, staring down at my house the night after Millicent's party, even the person Millicent had reported seeing in her yard…had those apparitions really been Victoria prowling the neighborhood dressed in Arthur's clothes?

"And the watch," Arthur went on. "Taking that watch off the skeleton was the last straw. She'd started going into that cellar, especially after those kids moved the old couch in there. I told Darla to keep checking there, but somehow Mother got in the cellar again and found the watch."

I shuddered. I couldn't stop myself. "You mean she took the watch off the skeleton?"

"She wanted it in the worst way. She thought a man she liked had given it to another girl instead of giving it to her. Maybe it was the wrong thing to do, but I told her she could keep it if she promised never to wear it. Then she did wear it. Darla saw her with it on." He began to cough in great, discordant barks which turned into spasms of choking as he struggled to catch his breath.

"Arthur, I'm so sorry about all this. But you've got to get out of here. I'm scared for you." I didn't add that I was scared for myself too. If Arthur passed out here in the mine, I'd be done for.

The coughing slowed and he seemed to pull himself together. "All right, Loren. I'll untie your feet. I can't carry you any further. I need to get to a place where the air is better."

Had I convinced him, or was he simply moving to the next phase of his plan? There was no way I could know for sure.

THIRTY

As Arthur was tugging me to my feet, his coughing spasms started again, but this time he got them under control quickly.

I stepped gingerly on first one foot and then the other. I wouldn't have thought I could hurt anymore, but now with pins and needles stabbing my legs and my injured knee throbbing even worse than it had before, my entire lower body screamed with pain.

Arthur moved up close behind me, grabbed a handful of my cover-up and shoved me along. My legs wobbled and, with my hands still tied behind me, I staggered from side to side as he prodded me down another corridor. I sensed we were going deeper into the mine.

"Arthur, you need to get to fresh air," I said.

"There's an exit this way. Keep going."

I didn't believe him.

As we picked our way along, the rocky surface we'd been walking on disappeared. There was sand beneath our feet now, and I careened from one side of the narrow passageway to the other, in constant danger of losing my footing. The bare light bulbs hanging from wires far above our heads gave little light.

"This sand. I can hardly stay on my feet," I said as I banged into an outcropping of rock.

"Not sand—guano," Arthur said.

"What does that mean?" I asked.

"Droppings from the bats, of course. This is where they hibernate."

Something sour welled up in my throat. I started to retch. I lurched against the wall, bent almost double as my body was racked with dry heaves.

Could things get any worse? My spirits sank to a new low. I couldn't give up, I reminded myself. Wasn't I the one who yakked about not needing a man to rescue me, who insisted I could save myself?

As I forced my body into an upright position, I felt a slight movement near my right wrist. The rope binding my hands together in back of me slipped a little, just a fraction of an inch, nothing much, but a definite change. Maybe, just maybe…

"Arthur, are you sure this is the way out?" I asked.

He didn't answer.

The air in this passageway had a colder, damper feel as if we'd moved further underground. In the light of the flash, I could see strings of bare electric bulbs draped along the walls of the tunnels, but they weren't lighted here. The only illumination came from Arthur's big flashlight.

We'd trudged along for maybe fifteen minutes more when Arthur stopped. In one quick movement he swept the beam of his light toward the ceiling of the mine.

I looked up, following the arc of the light.

Dark bunches varying in size and shape hung from the walls and ceiling above us. They ballooned out away from the rocks like monstrous growths. I couldn't believe my eyes at first. I thought they were playing tricks on me, but those bunches were moving, undulating, their shapes pulsating, their outlines changing ever so slightly. I couldn't figure out what they were. I'd never seen anything like them before.

The realization came slowly—bats, they were clusters of bats—sometimes only three to six small forms in a cluster, sometimes more than a dozen in a larger mass. Hundreds of them, maybe even thousands, huddled together. A few, disturbed by Arthur's light, writhed as if in protest, emitting high-pitched squeaks.

"Arthur, is this where they hibernate?" I backed against the wall of the tunnel, pressing my hands against the rocks until I hit a rough outcropping. If I could keep moving my hands against something like this, I might be able to cut through my bonds. I seesawed the ropes back and forth across the rock with as much pressure as I could manage. With the light concentrated on the ceiling, I was surrounded by thick shadows. I realized this might be my only chance.

We'd entered Arthur's element here. He wanted to

tell me about this world he studied and cared so passionately about, and I wanted him to. Anything to keep him from watching me too closely until I could saw through the ropes holding my arms.

"Just imagine it, Loren. There are hundreds of clusters like this, not only in this corridor, but all through the mine. These bats can lower their body temperature to match their surroundings. Isn't that amazing? They're subsisting now on the fat they stored when they were gobbling mosquitoes during the summer."

"Do you mean they'll stay here now for the rest of the winter? They've stored enough food for all those months?" I was surprised by what he was telling me. I didn't have to pretend.

"If they're not disturbed, they'll be all right. If they're roused, they use up those reserves."

"There's so many of them. I had no idea."

"We've been counting them the last couple of weeks," Arthur continued, apparently pleased by my interest. "At least we counted them as best we could. You know there can be more bats in one Adirondack mine than in all of New England and New Jersey together." He moved forward along the corridor, prodding me to go ahead of him.

"You've finished counting?" I asked. Did that mean no one else would be coming back to the mine? I'd told Don I didn't need a rescuer, sure, but one bat counter wouldn't be too much to ask for, would it?

Arthur warmed to the topic. "We completed the count two days ago. We do very careful calculations every few years, one of the ways we keep track of migrations."

I waited until we stopped again to ask more questions. I leaned back against the wall and shifted my hands until I found another outcropping of stone. "What if those bats start flying around? Aren't they rabid?"

"Very few. That's one of the many myths about bats, Loren. The ones you see here are mostly brown bats, very common to this area. Altogether, there are five different species in this one mine."

I strained harder against the ropes, forcing myself to move my arms up and down as fast as I could against the sharp edge of rock. The ropes burned and scraped the flesh under them.

"But they bite sometimes, don't they?"

"We're a lot more dangerous to them than they are to us," Arthur went on. "When a bat has to defend itself during hibernation, it uses up energy it needs to get through the winter, and it can die. If we see one moving, somebody yells 'flier' and we get out of its way."

"So we really shouldn't be in here disturbing them, should we? We ought to go," I said.

"This is the world they live in, Loren. You have to see it." He reached out quickly and switched off his light.

We were plunged into darkness. My throat closed

tight the same way it had when he pressed the pillow down on my face. I felt as if someone was strangling me. My heartbeat clanged in my ears. Darkness encompassed everything.

"Arthur, put the light back on," I gasped.

"You're in the bats' world now, Loren. This is as black as black gets. But there's life here. Listen."

The darkness magnified the sounds of the mine—the dripping of water on a nearby wall, the faint, intermittent chitterlings of the bats, the dull thud of a rock tumbling down an incline somewhere nearby.

"Arthur, please. I can't stand this." I choked on the words. This was my nightmare world, this cavernous empty space, devoid of light, peopled with monstrous terrors.

He didn't answer, but to my relief, he turned the flashlight back on. He began to shine the light up and down over the walls in a jigsaw pattern. Some of the bats squeaked in protest before he focused the beam high up on the wall, on a bat so pale in color that it dangled like a small, white ghost in the darkness.

"Look there, Loren, see that. It's an albino. It's been in this same place now three years in a row. Imagine that. It finds its way back, not just to this mine, but to this very spot every year."

"An albino bat? You mean it has no color? I never knew there was such a thing. It can find its way back to that same spot every year?" I repeated his words back to him, anxious to keep him talking while I rubbed my hands against the wall. Under different circumstances, I might have wanted to know more.

"Many of the other bats do the same thing—return to the exact place each fall. The albino's easy to pick out, so we always notice him."

"How can they do that? It seems impossible." Finally, I felt the ropes loosen and start to fall away. My hands ached as the blood rushed into them

"I told you, Loren, bats are very intelligent—like dolphins."

I grabbed for the ropes, coiling them loosely around my wrists. I wanted him to think my hands were still tied. But now what? I had no weapon. With my knee hurting so, I doubted I could outrun Arthur even if I could figure how to get out of the mine.

"Remember what this tunnel looks like, Loren. You may be the last person to see it. They're going to close off this section of the mine."

"Close it off? You mean close up the tunnel like you said they've done other places? But what about these bats? What will happen to them?"

"I'm glad you asked that question. Some people wouldn't, you know. In some places they blow up the entrance to a tunnel and leave the bats to die in there."

"How awful," I said. "Your group wouldn't do that, would they?"

"No. We have gates already built. They're made of

steel bars with open spaces between them, and they're ready to put up. They'll fit tight across the entrance to two of these tunnels. We'll cement them in. People won't be able to get through them, but the bats can fly in and out without a problem."

Fear formed deep in my gut and began spreading outward. I could feel my legs get weaker, my shoulders and arms begin to tremble. Did he mean to kill me or leave me to die in here, in a place where no one could come in? Was that why he'd brought me here?"

Arthur, his grip tight on my arm, shoved me toward the center of the large open space. We'd entered a cavern of some kind, a section of the ceiling arched even higher here, almost out of sight. He stepped more carefully now, his light focused on the ground ahead of us.

I pulled up short. In the glare of the flash, I saw a black, gaping hole yawning in front of us, a stinking pit, filled with brackish water, measuring at least twenty feet across, lined with jagged rocks. I couldn't see very far into it, couldn't tell how deep it was. At some point the area had been fenced off, but now at least half the posts, along with the rusted wires that had been strung between them, lay piled in heaps in the dirt.

Suddenly I knew. I knew what Arthur Blake had in store for me. I'd be Roberta Canfield all over again, shoved into a hell from which there was no escape and, if I survived the fall, abandoned there helpless in the darkness of that black pit, left to struggle desperately to stay alive for who knew how long, and finally to drown.

Time had run out. I had to make my move.

I took stock quickly. I had only two things I could use to my advantage—the rope and the element of surprise. I twisted the rope around my right hand, turned fast and swung a hard punch at Arthur's nose. The rope cushioned the blow a little for me, but my hand throbbed with pain as if I'd broken it.

Arthur staggered backward, blood spurting from his nose, his upper lip split with an ugly gash. He held on to the flashlight, but it swung wildly back and forth as he struggled to right himself. The beam raked the roof of the mine. A line of white streaked across the space above us.

I reached down and grabbed one of the fence posts. The wire fencing was still attached to it, but I wrenched the post toward me and gripped it tight. This wasn't like that night in the center when I planned to stun the shadowy form in the doorway with the flowerpot and run for my car. This time I'd have to hit someone, someone I knew, with enough force to maim or kill him. Could I really do that? The answer was clear. If I wasn't ready to die myself, I'd have to.

But Arthur had his own plan for me and he hadn't given up on it. He let out a frightening bellow of pain and frustration and pulled a gun from his pocket. Not a big gun—I couldn't tell what kind it was or what caliber—but it didn't matter. All he had to do was incapacitate me, injure me enough so he could throw me into that pit.

I gripped my fence post, determined to swing it with every ounce of strength I could muster.

Before I could make my move, the streak of white changed course and hurtled down from the roof of the mine, aiming straight at us.

Arthur himself had told me what to do.

So I did it.

"Flyer!" I cried.

Arthur saw the bat then and lunged back, trying to give it space. The albino, disoriented by the light, swooped directly toward him. Arthur's response was automatic. He scrambled back farther, trying to get out of the bat's line of flight.

But he'd lost track of where he was. He lurched sideways, straight into the rotting barricade. The wood split with a sickening crack. His arms flailed while he tottered closer to the edge of the pit. The flashlight flew out of his hand as he staggered backward, struggling to regain his balance. With one last horrifying scream, he plunged into the pit.

The flashlight went out. The darkness paralyzed me. I knew he'd fallen, but maybe he'd hung on somehow. Maybe he was already crawling out to come after me. My whole body began to shake.

But I'd come too far to give up now. I forced myself

to calm down and try to visualize where the flashlight had landed. I dropped to the ground, inching forward on my good knee, feeling for the hard casing of the flashlight, patting ahead of me with every movement to be sure I wasn't too close to the edge of the pit. I thought an eternity had gone by when my fingers bumped the flashlight's smooth metal case.

I picked it up gently, cradled it in my arms before I pushed the switch. Mercifully, the light came on, a little dimmer than it had been maybe, but there was a beam of light.

I edged my way over to the pit and peered down. Arthur lay sprawled across rocks, his face and upper body submerged in the water, easily thirty feet below where I was standing. He wasn't moving, wasn't trying to lift his head. He didn't seem to be breathing. There was no way I could reach him.

The albino bat fluttered back and forth over the pit as if unable to gain enough altitude to return to its roost. At least it had a better chance of surviving than Arthur. And unless I could find my way back to a lighted tunnel before the flashlight battery went dead, that bat's chances of staying alive were probably a lot better than mine.

THIRTY-ONE

EVERY INSTINCT URGED ME to take off as fast I could and keep running until I found my way out of that place. So maybe it was a good thing I couldn't run, couldn't even walk without stopping to rest my leg after every few steps. I was forced to calm down and figure out what to do.

The fence post I'd grabbed was too heavy to carry for long, but thinner pieces of wood were scattered around near the pit. I tested a couple until I found one that was a good length for a makeshift cane and thick enough to lean on. Then I started limping slowly back, hoping I was headed toward the lighted tunnel we'd come through.

I must have been due for some good luck because a few minutes later I stumbled on a track and a broken rail car similar to those I'd seen on the way in. I fought back the feeling there could be dozens of these ruined cars abandoned in the mine and decided this was the same one we'd passed a short time before.

Despite the searing pain in my left leg, I kept forcing myself to put one foot ahead of the other. I established a pattern: two or three steps leaning hard on the stick, then a short break, then repeat. No long stops, no sitting down to rest, no speculating on what might have happened to Josie, no thoughts about what would happen to me if I couldn't find my way out of here. I could do this. I had to.

When I finally saw a lighted tunnel ahead of me, my spirits lifted. Now I found it easier to keep to my routine. A few steps, rest, move on. I felt as if I'd been walking for hours. I couldn't tell how much time had passed, couldn't be sure if the turns I'd taken were leading me out of the mine or deeper into it, but finally I sensed a gradual brightening of the tunnel. I forced my legs to move faster, prayed my eyes weren't playing tricks on me, and finally I saw it. The arch of the mine entrance, blazing with white light, loomed in the distance.

The light. I'd never experienced anything like that light as I limped out of the mine into a world I'd thought I might never see again. Sunlight, so dazzling it forced me to shade my eyes, beat down all around me. The Adirondack sky, the most glorious blue I'd ever seen, arched over bushes flecked with reds and yellows so bright I could hardly look at them. The scrubby little pines around the parking area swayed gently in a soft breeze, as elegant as any oaks or maples.

Arthur's car was parked near the entrance. I tried the doors. They were locked tight. I told myself it was just as well. I wasn't sure I could have gotten into it.

I hobbled down the rutted dirt road to the highway, following the same pattern I'd set for myself in the mine—two or three steps, rest, two or three more. My leg screamed with pain, my head throbbed, but I could handle it all now. The long trek over the uneven ground exhausted me even more, but it offered a visual feast like nothing I'd ever experienced before.

I stopped finally when I reached pavement and signaled frantically to the first car to come by. I couldn't believe anyone would stop and pick up such a disreputable-looking hitchhiker, but I had to try. To my relief, a middle-aged man slammed on his brakes in response to my wave.

"Mayor Graham? Is that you?" he called.

"Thank you. Thank you for stopping. But who are you? How do you know me?"

"I'm Bruce Henderson," he explained. "I'm in and out of Emerald Point a lot on business. I've seen you there. Have you been in an accident? Tell me what I can do to help."

"I've got to call 911. There's somebody in that mine up there who needs the rescue squad—if it's not too late."

"My cell doesn't work here, but there's a store right down the road. I'll take you there," he said

Before I could ease myself into his front seat, another car, its horn blaring and lights flashing, pulled off the road in front of us. Josie Donohue tumbled out of the driver's side.

For the first time that day I couldn't hold back my tears. Tears of gratitude, of relief, of thanksgiving. "Josie, are you all right?" I sobbed.

"Lor, wait up. I figured this might be where you were. I was right, wasn't I? Was it Arthur? Did he bring you here? Who's this guy? Are you hurt? You look awful. Tell me."

A crushing weight dropped from my shoulders. Even the pain in my knee began to ease a little. "Josie, are you really all right? How did you know to come here?"

"I'll tell you in a minute. Let's call 911 first. We'll get a deputy up here. And how about the emergency squad too? You look like you need a doctor." Josie held her cell phone in front of her, ready to make the calls.

I turned back to Bruce. "Thank you anyway. This young lady will take care of me now."

And she did.

THIRTY-TWO

"YOU'RE A REAL Florence Nightingale," I told Josie Donohue that evening as I lay on the couch in my living room, numbed by pain pills and a steady barrage of questions from sheriff's deputies and EMTs.

"Who's Florence Nightingale?" she asked as she re-arranged the pillows she'd packed around me.

"It's a major compliment. Just accept it," I said.

As she busied herself plumping another pillow, Don and I exchanged smiles. He'd stayed by my side all afternoon, acting as go-between with the sheriff's deputies and the rescue squad, and staying in touch with the bat counters and the other volunteers who'd gone into the mine to retrieve Arthur's body.

Earlier, Josie had taken time off from her nursing duties to tell the deputies how she'd been lured away the night before. She'd been asleep on my living room couch when the phone wakened her around five o'clock. The caller had given a name she didn't recognize and insisted her mother wanted her to come straight home.

"She was in an accident and she needs you to drive her to the emergency room," the voice had insisted.

So Josie, frantic about Kate, had checked on me, seen that I was asleep and rushed off. To her surprise, she found her mother in perfect health and mystified about the call. When it dawned on her that she'd been tricked, she rushed back and found me gone.

"I wasted a ton of time," she said when we compared notes on our experiences. "I went to Arthur Blake's house. It was the first place I thought of because you'd been with Mrs. Blake in the cellar. Darla What's-Her-Name insisted that Arthur was still in bed and she couldn't help me. I finally talked her into checking his room and he wasn't there. Then I got the idea he might have taken you to the hospital or something like that."

So she'd made other calls—to the hospital, to Don, to her friends who hung out in the cellar, and finally, as she began to suspect I was in trouble and Arthur was somehow responsible for it, to the sheriff's department.

"As soon as it hit me that Arthur might be the bad guy in this, I told the sheriff's department everything I knew, but I didn't wait around for them to start moving on it. I made tracks fast up to the mine where he hangs out."

"Good detective work," I said, and tried not to think about what might have happened to her if she'd followed Arthur and me into the mine.

To everyone's astonishment, Doc Tarrington made a house call to check me out. After he finally succumbed to my pleas to skip the Emergency Room, he prescribed pain medicine, wrapped my aching knee, sprained ankle and torn wrists and sent Don to the kitchen to make cold packs for all other injured parts.

Then, like the great guy he was, he agreed to go with one of the deputies to break the news about Arthur's death to his mother.

"Well, I did it," he told Don and me with a shudder an hour later when he returned to my house. "She was devastated, of course, but I'm not sure how much she'll remember. She seems very clear about some things, then she slips back into the past."

"What will happen to her now without Arthur? He was the one responsible for her, wasn't he?" I said.

"I told that woman with her—Darla, is it?—not to leave her alone until someone makes arrangements for her. And we won't know for a while what they'll be. I doubt she can be charged with anything after all these years, but I don't think she can stay on in the house, even if she had somebody staying with her. She'll probably have to go into some kind of nursing facility."

The very thing Arthur had wanted to avoid.

A few minutes after Doc left, a weary-looking Investigator Thompson followed Don into the living room and pulled up a straight chair near the couch.

"You feel like talking, Mayor?" he asked.

"Sure. But tell me what you found at the mine. I assume that's where you were."

"Bad scene there. We had to get equipment in to raise Arthur's body out of that pit. Took a long time."

I shuddered. It could have been my body he was talking about.

Jim pulled out his notebook. "We don't have to spend all night on this. I know you've both told the deputies what happened. I just want confirmation."

Josie was happy to explain her role again, and Jim listened carefully, even nodded approvingly from time to time. "Up until the point you rushed up to that mine ahead of the deputies, you handled things well, Josie. If you just hadn't done that…"

Josie, speechless for once, stared at him in disbelief.

When Jim turned his attention to me, I felt surprisingly calm. I didn't expect to get an accolade like Josie's, but the pain pills had left me too mellow to worry.

I described what had happened to me, at least everything I remembered.

To my surprise, Jim didn't explode. "Deputy Cronin's beating himself up for telling Arthur some of what you said about his mother's behavior in the cellar. Never dreamed he would react the way he did."

"Does that mean you're not going to find a way to pin this whole thing on me?" I asked him.

"Don't push it. I may just be relieved I didn't have to watch them fish you out of that pit along with Arthur Blake."

It must have been the drugs Doc had given me, because I didn't say anything in response to that statement. I let Jim Thompson have the last word.

AFTER JIM AND JOSIE LEFT, Don made me a sandwich from some leftovers he found in the refrigerator and insisted I go to bed.

"I think you've had enough excitement for one day," he said as prepared to carry me upstairs.

"I can think of something that would make my day more exciting," I told him.

He eyed me suspiciously. "So can I, but I don't think you're up to it."

"I meant if I got engaged," I said.

"Engaged?"

"To be married."

"And who would you get engaged to?"

"To you, of course. Isn't your offer still open?"

"Here I thought my proposal to you was unromantic. Yours is even worse."

So then I broke down and told him some of the things I'd thought about in the mine—about how I might never see him again and never get a chance to make a life with him. I told him how I finally realized that I often took chances for stupid reasons, but shied away from taking them on the things that really mattered.

Then I apologized, actually said the words for once. And I didn't do it as a last resort, but because I

really was sorry I hadn't been smart enough to see
what life would be like without him. I even used the
L word, not just once, but a couple of times, and it
wasn't anywhere near as hard to say as I thought it
would be.

And we got engaged.